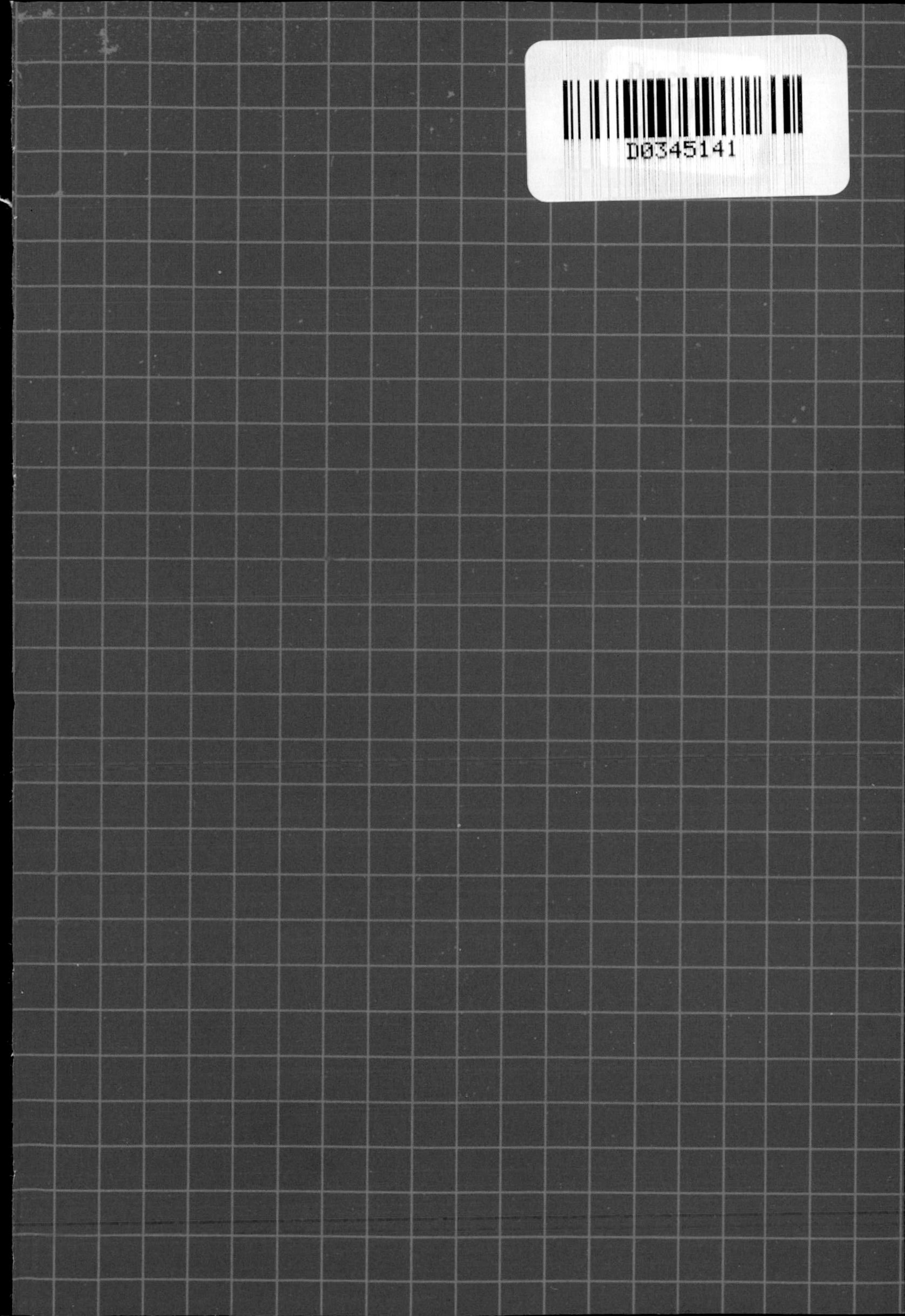

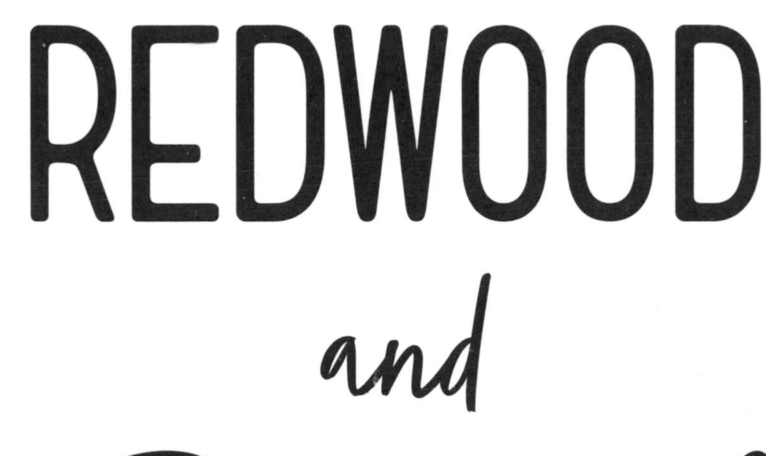

K.A. Holt

chronicle books · san francisco

Library of Congress Cataloging-in-Publication Data available.

ISBN 978-1-4521-7288-0

Manufactured in China.

Design by Jennifer Tolo Pierce.
Typeset in Really No 2 LT CYR.

10 9 8 7 6 5 4 3 2 1

Chronicle Books LLC
680 Second Street
San Francisco, California 94107

Chronicle Books—we see things differently.
Become part of our community at
www.chroniclekids.com.

For my wife, Shannon.

NOW

Alex	Alyx	Alexx
We are the kids in the halls . . .		
	We are the kids you don't see . . .	
		We are the kids watching . . .
We are everyone.		
	We are everywhere.	
		We are everything.
And what do we see?		
	And what do we see?	
		And what do we see?
A love story?		
	A tragedy?	
		A comedy?
Real life?		
	Will we cry?	
		Will we laugh?
I guess we'll find out.		
	I guess we'll find out.	
		I guess we'll find out.

Our quest for
normal . . .

Our search for
truth . . .

Our all-knowing
glances . . .

always watching her.

always watching him.

always watching you.

<table>
<tr><td>

TAM

I dig the heel of my palm
calmly pressing
into my chest
harder and harder
because I know it's there
it has to be
somewhere
beating

</td><td>

Kate

I stare out the window
the sun huge
bright
burning
taking up the whole sky
and it's like
I can see inside
my chest

</td></tr>
<tr><td colspan="2" align="center">

my heart

my heart

my heart

</td></tr>
<tr><td>

So why does it feel
missing
skipping
every
beat
nothing alive
inside me?

Could it be
that my palm digs calmly
because you can't panic
when you have no
beats?

</td><td>

Bursting
too full
it hurts
so much
all the feelings
pressed into my ribs
like my eyes to the window.

Could it be
that all the feelings
are exploding
at once, finally
free?

</td></tr>
</table>

my heart

my heart

my heart

Where are you?
Where could you be?
Why would you leave me here
so quiet
so empty?

Why are you like this?
Why do this to me?
Why aren't you
normal?
Why can't you leave me be?

• •

TAM

What does it mean
to be a friend?

I ask this question
to my ceiling
quietly,
a whisper
with no answer.

• •

Kate

In my pocket,
a book.

Not a regular book;
a tiny book that tells my future.

I take it,
open it.

Inside, lined up in two rows,
faceless, armless
matches. Fates.

They know the way.

• •

TAM

I miss her.
Every part of me.
Every molecule.
But this is what she wants.
So this is my gift to her.
Leaving her alone.
Going away.

My present is
zero presence.
Exactly what she wants.

• •

Kate

The match explodes,
a burst of light
and sulfur.

I hold it to the poster
pinned to my wall.
The poster that started it all.

I understand now
why people say
flames lick
because I see the orange tongue
slide up the side,
slurping the paper,
eating its glowing snack.

Black
smoke also licks,
leaving a mark on the ceiling
while I watch everything
burn.

Katherine?

Mom barges in.

KATHERINE?

The smoke alarm
bright in my ears:
Beep-beep! Beep-beep! Beep-beep!

Katherine!
What are you—?
Get the—!
Oh my G—!

Mom tries to push me
out out out of the room
but I don't budge.
She runs past me,
shouts,

Where's the fire extinguisher?!

And in my chest
everything lurches,
comes alive
pounds
beats
a new pulse
matching the alarm.

The poster burns.
I hold out my phone.
I hit record.
Flames lick, devour,
reach golden arms to the ceiling.

And my eyes
close.
I feel the heat.
I breathe the ash.
As a new chapter
in the story of my future

begins

right

now.

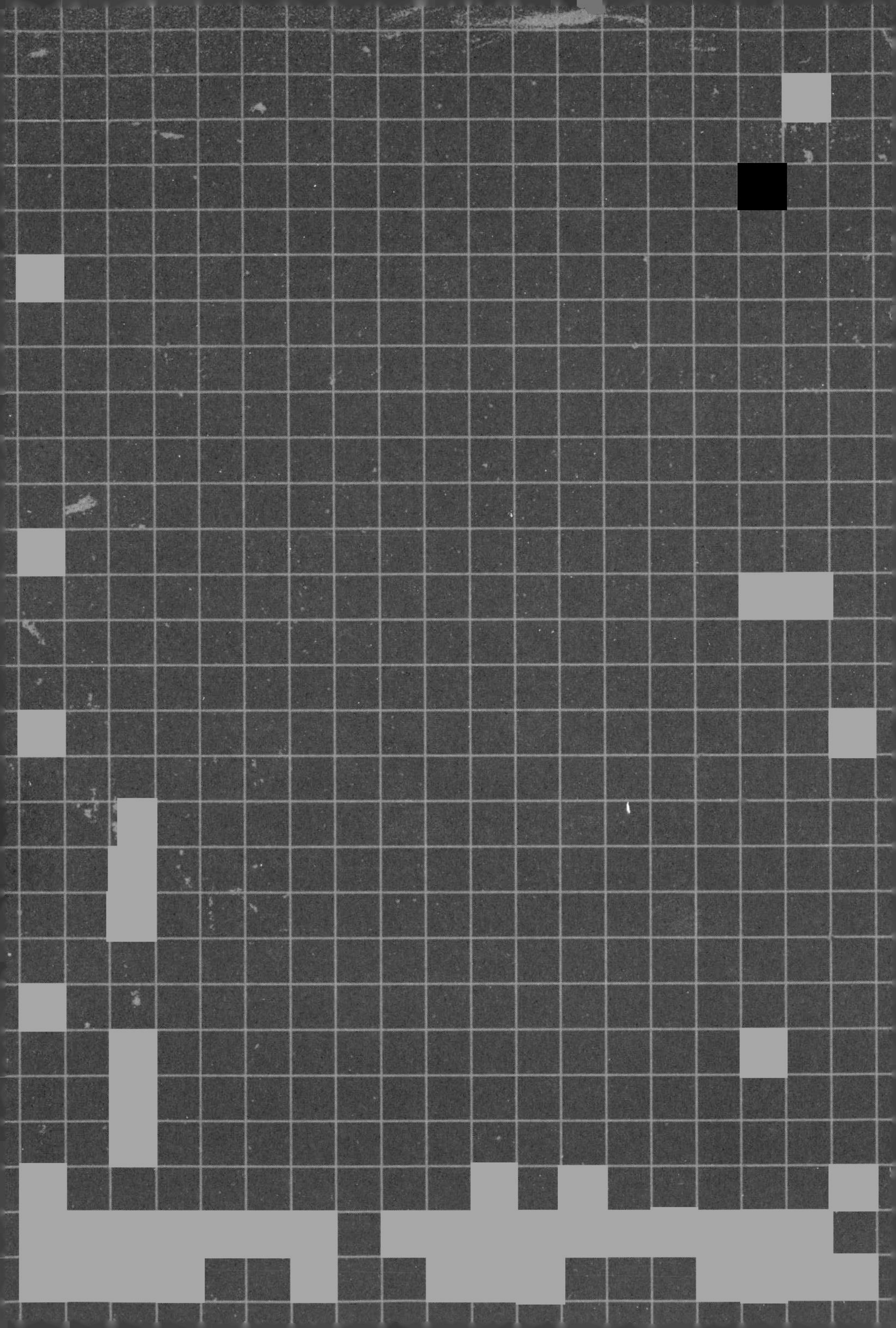

BEFORE

Kate

Just right.

I tell myself this
as I straighten my bow,
smooth my skirt,
tie my shoes.

You're just right.

Breathe in.
Breathe out.

Bow tight.
Smile bright.
Just right.

• •

TAM

Like a breeze
or a sneeze
you blink
and it's over.

How does that happen?
I mean, really?
Summer is here
and then it's gone.
Snatched away
and before you know it
it's registration day,
new schedules,
new classes,
and I don't hate the idea
of school back in session,
but really
does *anyone*
love it?

• •

Kate

I love it!
At least I think I do.
I always *have* loved it,
so surely this year will be the same.
School itself is neither here nor there
but all the kids and clubs and stuff?
That's the fun part.
Right?

It always has been.
So I'm sure it will be that way
this year, too.

Almost ready?

Born ready, Mom.

Tell that to my watch.

Mom's smile
is a little bit sideways when we get to the car,
a troublemaker grin I recognize
from someone else's face,
a grin I haven't seen in a long time.

For your birthday.

She hands me an envelope,
and what?
My birthday is so far away!
I tilt my head, like a confused puppy.
Mom laughs.

Look inside.
You'll understand.

I open the envelope
and oh my gosh,
so many tickets . . .

Mom!

She laughs again.

MisDirection is playing?!
ON MY BIRTHDAY?!

I know, honey.
I bought enough tickets for
the whole squad.
How could I not?

The whole squad invited
to a concert
on my birthday?
It'll be amazing . . .

Mom smiles, taps her temple.

Always thinking ahead.

Right.
I should be cheer captain by then
and if I'm not,
these will seal the deal.

• •

Kate

I make my hand into a microphone,
I sing,
Oh, baby,
Oh, baby,

Mom puts the car in reverse,
turns to look behind her,
backs out of the driveway,
eyes focused,
smile tight now,
tight as my bow.

And this smile,
the familiar one,
not the lopsided one,
the all-knowing,
all-seeing
Mom-smirk . . .
it makes my stomach flip
just a tiny smidge.

I keep looking at Mom,
I croon into my hand
softer this time:

Oh, baby,
Don't,
Don't,
Don't break my heart in two.

Because yeah,
I'm happy about the tickets
but also?
Does everything,
even my *birthday*
have to be a chess move?

• •

TAM

Are you stoked for school?

Mom. Please don't say stoked.

Don't be shook, baby.
I'm sure it will be very lit.

Mom. No. Never say those words.

We're both laughing now
as the car wheezes up to
school
and the radio kicks in
with ridiculous bass
and that stupid song
Oh, Baby
starts up
and my ears,
they bleed.

Ahhh! No!! It's too much!
Between you and this,
just . . .
turn it off!
Turn you off!

Mom cackles her witch laugh,
pulls to the curb at school:

Oh, baby,
oh, baby,
how I love yoooooou.
Please, baby, please,
don't break my heart in
twoooooo.

STOPPPPPPPP!

I jump out,
slam the car door,
laughing even though it
encourages her.

See you later!

I can still hear Mom singing
as she drives off.

• •

Kate

Becca's scream is so loud,
so long,
so piercing,
I'm afraid for a minute
she's going to turn herself
inside out.

MisDirection?!
ALL of us?!
LOVE YOUR MOM!!!!

Seriously, I think she might cry.
And for some reason
her enthusiasm,
her made-for-TV freak-out,
it just,
I don't know,
oh, baby,
oh, baby,
how I wishhhhhhhh
I'd kept the secret
a little bit longer.

Is that weird?
I don't know.

• •

TAM

Juggernaut-less gym
today.
No whistles.
No squeaks.
No leaping and landing,
digging and diving.
Instead,
pencils and schedules,
sighs and lines.
Registration day.
Seventh grade.

I look up at the caged bulbs,
big round bright,
they heave
fluorescent sighs
coughing out light on
one table at a time.
Find my line
A through *F*
whisper an apology
to the lights:

Tomorrow night,
first practice.
It'll be more fun in here,
I promise.
Volleyballs
whizzing by,
no tables
no signs
no pencils
in sight.

• •

Kate

Fingers sticky from all the tape,
I smooth my skirt,
survey the gym.
It looks fine.
Better than fine.
It looks fabulous.
So why does everything feel . . .
so much the same?

Kate.
Kate?
My MisDirection Queen?

Hey.
Earth to Kate.

Can you help with this bunting?
It's collapsing under its own weight.

My smile,
can it be fake *and* sincere?
Is that even a thing?
Hmm?
I say.
Bunting? I'll be right there, okay?

Welcome back, sheep,
don't you all look so fluffy
and pretty
today.

• •

TAM

Levi.
My happy little flea
boink boink boink
bouncing
around the gym
saying hi to everyone.
We've been friends since kinder
and he's always been the one
who knows my sentences
before I say them,
who laughs at my jokes
when they're super dumb.
My kid,
my pal,
my shortstack,
my man about town.
Levi, Levi.
I can count on him
cause he's always around.

Hey, nerd!

Hey, turd!

How's my man's man,
ladies' man,
man about town?

Juuuust fine.
How's the reigning volleyball
champion of the world?

Juuuuust fine.

We high-five
low-five
fake-out five
then someone waves,

Hey, Levi!

and he's off.
King of the school,
strutting his stuff,
my favorite goof,
my shortstack bud.

• •

Kate

Mom would love this.
She really would.
The girls surrounding me,
singing,
so thrilled for the concert.

It's like everyone is here today
to see *me*
to talk to *me*
to hang out with *me*.
Registration is . . . secondary.

• •

TAM

Over there
strutting,
laughing,
she thinks I don't see
but I do,
I do,
that little cheerleader
looking at me.
The red bow in her hair
snapped military tight,
right?

Like she must've used a ruler
and glue
and maybe an iron, too,
to get that perfect
swoop
on top of a perfect
swinging
ponytail
like I've never seen,
swish swish
catching the light,
blinding my eyes,
that snappy red bow,
those bright highlights
like
what
excuse me
what
are you on purpose
bringing every clichéd cheerleader
to life?

• •

Kate

This girl in the gym today,
looking at me.
Tall as a palm tree,

shaped like one, too.
Big hair on top,
giraffe neck,
legs like a stick figure
stretching right off the page,
her skin shimmering
her head tossed back
a loud laugh flying from her mouth
while a boy
small as she is tall
bounces around her feet
making her see
nothing in the world but
him.

• •

Alex	Alyx	Alexx
Alex, Alyx, Alexx.		
	Chillin' in the shadows.	
		Watching everything.
Watching everything.		
	Alex, Alyx, Alexx.	
		Chillin' in the shadows.
Chillin' in the shadows.		
	Watching everything.	
		Alex, Alyx, Alexx.
We see all.		
	Hear all.	
		Know all.
We know all.		
	See all.	
		Hear all.
We hear all.		
	Know all.	
		See all.
We three queens.		
	We three queens.	
		We three queens.

Kate

And just like that
we tear it all down.
No more bunting.
No more signs.
Fold up the tables.
The gym is now a
gym again.

Practice in ten!

Coach herds us to
the locker room.

Mom is right.
The squad will love
me as captain.
I close my eyes.
I can see it.
I will make it happen.

Okay, everyone. I need a favor.

Coach, in her office,
holding . . .
what is that?
A giant dead bird?

Mitchell Phresch moved away
and we have no mascot,
at least until we have tryouts,
at least for the first few games.

The pause is so long,
with giggles here and there.

Who wants to volunteer?

No one raises their hand
and I can't blame them.
That dead bird,
probably hot,
probably smelling
like Mitchell (not so) Phresch.

But you know what?
I hear Mom's voice in my head:
I could *take one for the team.*
Why not?
Everyone will love me more,
and when it comes time
I'm captain
Bam
no other choice.

I raise my hand.

I'll do it.

Well all right, Katherine!
Way to step up.

The girls all giggle.
Becca raises her hand.

Yes, Becca?

But the mascot . . .
it's not
part of the squad.

Technically, you're right.
But Kate is flexible.
She can straddle the line.

I laugh.
But inside I start to wonder.
Wait . . . what did I just do?

• •

TAM

Only one class with Levi.
That'll be weird.
But fine.
At least for me.

He,
that goofy doof,
seems worried.
Shortstack can hold his own,
though.
He'll be fine.
We'll be fine.
Still rulin' the school
one day at a time.

• •

Kate

I still have a little Falcon
in my step,
skipping home
though I'm back in my cheer uniform,
the picture of normal.

And can I just say?
Who knew being the mascot
could be so fun?
I flapped and ran
and leapt and spun
and yes it was sweaty
and yes it didn't smell great
but all in all
this turned out
to be a pretty fun day.

• •

TAM

Making my way home,
I see up ahead
that cheerleader from earlier
bouncing
bobbing,
sidewalk hopping.

I cross over the courts
to see what's what
when
this kid
wanders over,
palming a ball
dribbling words
like he's ten feet tall.

You want to play, son?

This kid with
baggy shorts
cropped hair
staring
at me,
crinkled eyes
sizing
me
up.

Bet you could hit a basket or two.

I let him talk,
keep my mouth shut
lips stuck
tight
as he dribbles
and squints.

Wanna play or what, dude?

I still don't talk;
slap the ball
right out of his hand
his squint lost
in surprise
when I bounce that ball high
off his forehead
then catch it
with one hand.
Walk away.

Hey! Ow! That's my ball!
What's your damage, man?

I don't turn around;
just drop the ball,
letting the ground
catch it
carry it away,
shaking
my head.

Yeah, I could hit a basket or two.
Yeah, I could play some ball.
But I'm not his son.
I'm not a man.
And just because
I'm wearing a snapback
and Chucks,
that doesn't mean I'm a dude.

• •

TAM

Kate

The little cheerleader
from earlier
saunters up,
eyes twinkling bright.

I get that all the time, you know.
Always mistaken for a dude.

Her half-smile
tickles my eyes.

Well I admit,
as soon as I saw you
I thought,
linebacker
for sure.
I smirk.

I roll my eyes.

She rolls her eyes.

Smirk.

She puts her hand on her hip.

I cock my hip to the side.

I try to be serious.
I try not to smile.

Wouldn't surprise me
if you were quite
the athlete.

She reaches over,
surprising *me*,
squeezes
my arm.

I squeeze
her tiny bird-bone arm,
but it's firm,
solid.
All muscle,
hidden
out of sight.

What's your name, Ponytail?

My name is Kate.
What's yours?
Redwood?

Cause I'm so tall?
Hilarious.
My name is Tam.
Short for Tamara.
But I have to put you through that basket—
I point to the court—
if you
ever
call me Tamara.

Nice to meet you, Tam.

Nice to meet you, Kate.

I wink

She winks!

and I jog off.

• •

Alex	Alyx	Alexx
Like a Redwood.	She towers.	So glam.
So glam.	Like a Redwood.	She towers.
She towers.	So glam.	Like a Redwood.
Intriguing the Ponytail.	Intriguing the Ponytail.	Intriguing the Ponytail.
Perhaps.	A story.	In the making.
In the making.	Perhaps.	A story.
A story.	In the making.	Perhaps.
The Alexes take notice.	We extra notice.	You couldn't not notice.

TAM

Mom.
I laugh,
point.
Her chin faces the ceiling
like a yoga salute
and a gymnastics move
and an emoji
combined.

She laughs.
It's the thousandth time
she's worn her ID
upside down.

Oh, good grief.
I'm smiling up at me!

New scrubs?

She pats her thighs.
My special occasion scrubs.

When I look confused
she laughs again.

First day of seventh grade!

Wow, you're old for seventh grade.

Mom bops my head with a notepad.

Nervous?

Nah.

She gets
That Look,
clears her throat.
Her eyes peer
over the top
of her sparkly purple
glasses.

NERVOUS?

NAH.

She bops me again.

Have a great day, Love.
Remember, you only YOLO once.

I laugh.
Mom. No.
Don't try to be cool.

I'm totally cool.
I make you LOL out loud
all
the
time.

Mom. Stop.
Have a good day at work.

And then she hugs me
and I can see the top of her head,
silver tinsel
glittering in the black.

Your gift to me,
she always says,
silver in my hair
sparkle in my day.

• •

Kate

Just the right shade.
For the future cheer captain,
following in her mother's footsteps.

Mom presents lipstick,
it's in a small golden box.

My mom wouldn't let me wear lipstick
at your age. Isn't that crazy?

She smiles,
like we have a secret.
I take the box.
The lipstick is light pink.

You're so beautiful, Katherine.
The prettiest girl in school.

I roll the lipstick tube
across my palm.

Obviously,

she continues,

the smartest, most talented girl, too.
Just like her mom.

Weirdly, I want to throw
the box,
bounce it off her head
like Tam did with the ball
and that stupid kid.
But I don't.
I let her kiss my cheek.
I say,
Thank you.
I love you.
And as she shuts my door.
I put the lipstick,
unopened,
in my desk drawer.

• •

TAM

I'm not *nervous*
about the first day;
that's a thing
I don't get:
nervous.

I just see . . .
the buses lined up,
kids spewing out,

new boobs,
new hair,
new clothes.
Shouts
echo loud.

And I feel . . .
the same flutter
I get
before the first serve.
The shudder
up my neck
before the clock's numbers
blur.

There's no whistle right now,
just the bell,
piercing, short.
Here we go,
DaSilva.

Time
to
own
the
court.

• •

Kate

Mom says
I can rule them all.
Just like she did.
Cheer captain.
Smartest student.
Biggest future.
This is why I roam the halls,
chin high,
hair perfect,
smile bright.

The spotlight?
It's already
mine.

• •

TAM

It's so weird
not having Levi here.
I mean, he's *here,*
I know that,
but in different classes . . .
it's out of whack,
topsy-turvy.

And everywhere I go,
everywhere I look,
that cheerleader,
Ponytail
from registration day,
is all over the place,
like a speck caught in my eye.
Can't look away.
Can't blink her gone.
Can't figure her out.
It's like she came from nowhere,
blotting out the sun,
except she IS the sun.
Bright. Bright. Bright.
I squint in her direction,
wonder how Levi
is doing,
and she squints back
laughs,
making me feel as upside down
as Mom's ID badge.

• •

Kate

The first time we nodded.
The second time we smiled.
The third time we waved.
The fourth time we laughed.
Seriously.
Is that Tam girl in ALL my classes?

• •

TAM

Everywhere I look
there's Kate.
In class.
Kate.
In the hall.
Kate.
I close my eyes.
Kate.

• •

Kate

So here's a weird thing
that just happened
that I can't really explain.

I walked in the cafeteria,
saw our usual cheer table,
the one from last year
next to the window,
same view of the trees,
same dripping AC,
same everybody
over there
eating, noisy,
waving me over.

And on the other side of the room
I saw that girl Tam
and her little flea-sized friend.

I stopped in my tracks.

Sure, I could go to my friends,
sit and laugh.
Graham could pull my ponytail,
I could steal his chips.

I could ask Becca about camp,
she could borrow my pen.
But for some reason I thought:
nah.

Redwood's in, like,
all my classes, but
we haven't really had a chance
to chat, you know?
And I thought maybe
I'd like to say hi right now.
Is that strange?

Becca gestured at me,
from across the cafeteria,
lifting her shoulders
like she was asking
What are you doing?
But I pretended I didn't see her as
I dropped my tray on the table
across from Tam
and the boy
sparkling at her side.

I didn't look back at Becca.
Instead, I looked up.
I smiled.
Tam smiled back.

And now here we are,
sitting across from each other,
strangers
at lunch
together.

• •

TAM

She very carefully
unwraps
the plastic
exposing
her straw
and very carefully
pokes it
into her juice.
No drips.
No spray.
No spills.
No mess.

She very carefully
unwraps
the plastic
around
her sandwich,

leaving half of it covered
so her fingers
stay clean
and lettuce
doesn't spill.

She very carefully
takes a bite.
Rosy starburst lips
pinched tight
as she chews,
mouth closed.
She looks up.

What?

I look away.

• •

Kate

What?

She's staring.
Has she never seen
anyone eat
before?

I open my eyes wide
chew slower,
a rhino at the zoo.

She laughs.
I laugh.

In the background
Levi, sparkly flea boy,
is talking about . . .
something . . .
but I don't hear
over the staring
and the laughing,
a moment that only fits two.

• •

Alex	Alyx	Alexx
Two new friends, leaning close.		
	Redwood.	
		Ponytail.
Heads bowed.		
	Eyes staring.	
		Giggling and snorting.
Space bends around them.		
	Space bends around *her*.	
		Space bends around *her*.
Redwood and Ponytail.		
	Ponytail and Redwood.	
		The plot, as they say, thickens.

TAM

So you survived?
Levi rolls his eyes,
sighs,
doesn't want to talk.
Fine.

I mean,
I can tell
by his stiff shoulders,
his squinched mouth,
his gaze
distant
over the treetops . . .
I can tell
he wants to say something
but isn't talking.

I guess his first day
didn't go as well
as mine.

• •

Kate

Becca wants to know where I was
at lunch.
Becca wants to know why I didn't come over
at lunch.
Becca wants to know if something was wrong
at lunch.

I don't really want to talk about
lunch.

It was just . . .
lunch.
And I was just eating
lunch.
And Tam made me laugh at
lunch.

Lunch was lunch,
I tell Becca
while I tie my shoes for practice.
But she leans over me,
her eyes
her face
her half-frown
hungry
for more.

• •

TAM

Frankie?
Hello?

Tick tock
tick tock
kitchen clock
only sound
when I bound
through the door.

Frankie?
Where are you?

Tick tock
tick tock
kitchen clock
Mom still on shift,
so it's Frankie's house
after practice.

Out here!

Tick tock
tick tock
kitchen clock
I grab a soda,
grab a Swiss roll,
head out to the backyard.

Tick tock
tick tock
I half expect Kate
to walk through the door.

Have I even gone five seconds today
without seeing that cheerleader?

• •

TAM

I bet she didn't think
she'd be looking after me
all the time,
almost every day,
but here I am,
here I've always been,
born the day after she retired.

Frankie Little,
like a grandma,
but not related.
Next-door neighbor,
but so much more than that.
I call her my Neighma.
She calls me her Grandneighbor.

We are
our own
tiny
team.

• •

TAM

How is Meercat?

Better today.

Meercat blinks at me.
One slow blink, like I am
incredibly boring
or incredibly annoying.
He's one to talk.
He just sits there,
big fat lizard,
never moving.

How was your first day?

My brain rewinds,
flashing the day
behind my eyes.
All I see is that cheerleader
everywhere I turned,
getting in my way,
but not in a bad way.

I met this kid,
Kate.
She's in, like, all of my classes.
She's a cheerleader.
She has this ponytail.
You should see it.
Bouncing side to side
like she controls it with her mind.

Frankie looks at me
some classic side-eye,
just like Meercat.
The more she stays quiet,
the more I talk,
a signature move
of the Neighma Team.

• •

Kate

Chloe made a countdown clock
and shared it with the whole squad.
It's called
MDOMG,
counting down to the concert.

So then, of course,
everyone was distracted at practice
and Coach
was not
having
it.

She pulled me aside,
told me to rein them in.
She knows I want to be captain,
and she knows I can run the show.

So I put my foot down.
Told them to straighten up
or else forget MDOMG.
I'll donate the tickets to the homeless
if I have to.

And the rest of practice was smooth
because they know who's boss.
They know I'm right.

• •

Kate

Her nails tap on the wood,
reflecting in the gloss.
Her lips pucker;
I squint to see
if I reflect in *their* gloss.

She was not happy
when she saw the falcon head.
She was not happy when I stuffed it
in the car.
She was not happy I had not
told her earlier.
Her nails
continue
to
tap.

I don't love this, Katherine.

I don't either.
(Even though
I think
maybe I do.)

You know how busy I am, right?
With Dad out of town for work,
I have a million things to handle,
and this is NOT something
I'd planned to have on my list.

Dad has been out of town
"for work"
for months,
living in a new house,
but it feels like maybe
I shouldn't bring that up
right now.

You do realize . . .
only cheerleaders
can be cheer captains.
A mascot is NOT
part of the squad.

I know.
It's only temporary.

I am a little upset,
if I'm being honest.
Maybe I should call Coach.

No, Mom, please don't.
It's just for a game or two.
I'm taking one for the team,
like you always say.
They love me for it.
You should have seen me today,
I—

Of course they love you!
They aren't the ones
looking like fools.

I won't look like a fool.

You'll be wearing a falcon head
the size of a school bus.
Not a lot of art or skill in that,
Katherine.

Her nails keep tapping.
Her lips stay pursed.

You're the most athletic of them all.
This is ridiculous.
Though I will say,
I'm much less upset now,
to be missing the first few games.
You can act the fool
while I'm taking care of the remodel,
and then . . . back to business.
Back to campaigning for captain,
if the squad even remembers
who you are.

I'll be a giant falcon, Mom.
Not invisible.
It'll be fine.
They'll want *me to be captain.*
You should've seen—

We'll see.

There's a bang at the door.

Oh!

Mom's eyes light up.

The new flooring!
The delivery truck is here!

She jumps up,
kisses my head,
walks briskly away.

I pick up the falcon head,
its giant eyes stare at me.
Well, whew, dude.
Looks like we've got a few more
games together.

• •

TAM

Did I have a good day?
It felt mostly . . . the same.
But there was a tiny light
something different
I wonder
will it still be there tomorrow?
This new discovery
A lightness
A spark—

Kate

Did I have a good day?
It felt mostly . . . the same.
But there was something different
a little bit of light
I wonder
will it still be there tomorrow?
An unexpected lightness
A discovery
A spark?

Of something new.

• •

Alex

Alyx

Alexx

Have you heard?

Oh, I've heard.

Big news, big news.

A new mascot.

A concert.

Big news, big news.

Have you seen?

Oh, I've seen.

Bigger news,
bigger news.

A shake-up at lunch.

Tables asunder.

The *only* news.

Kate

I heard her before I saw her,
that echoing laugh
turning the corner
before those long legs
strode into view.
And when she spun by
she gave me a high five
even though she never stopped
moving,
and I
felt the sting on my palm
as I watched her rush by,
little Levi
nipping at her heels.

I hear a snap snap snap
as I touch my burning palm
and Becca yells,

Yearbook!

as her camera flashes,
this moment caught,
like a Tuesday morning butterfly,
held tight.

• •

TAM

When I get here early, I do a spin
from hall to hall
locker to locker
just to see who's in,
just to say hi,
cause why sit still
if you can fly?

Today we flew,
Levi and I,
beating the bell,
knocking shoulders,
slapping high fives
and I came around the corner,
catching Kate off guard,
smacking her hand hard
and laughing at her surprise,
her ow-shaped mouth.

Then I realized my own hand
still stung,
a zinging, singing redness
from when our palms smacked,
and I could still feel its warmth
even once I got to class.

• •

TAM

Oh no she did not.
I spin in my desk.
She waves from the back.
I point at her.
She smiles and shrugs.
That little Ponytail
just smacked my head,
right when she walked by,
an open palm to the skull
like I'm the volleyball.
Girl.
I am untouchable.
Everyone knows that.
But Ponytail just smirks and waves,
so confident she can get away with it.

• •

Kate

I mean, how could I resist?
She smacked my hand,
I smack her head.
Redwood's sitting down,
so it's the only time
I can reach it.

And oh the look on her face
when she sees it's me.
Her shock turns to
surprise.
I love that this girl
who knows everyone and everything
still can't figure me out.

• •

Kate

Another day, another sandwich.
I scan the cafeteria.
Cheer table: the same everything.
Tam's table: empty.
Cheer table: still the same everything.
Tam's table: still empty.
Becca waves me over.
No Tam in sight.
Cheer table, it is.

Where've you been?

What's up, Kate?

We've missed you!

We all chat,
it's just like always,
my crew, my squad.
Except, I don't know . . .

it's like eating pizza when
you're craving cake.
Fine, but not satisfying.
Fun, but not what I want.

I scan the room for Tam.
I chew a bite of sandwich.
The clock ticks slowly.
Cheerleader Kate stays
on display.

• •

TAM

Yes, I let Levi climb me like a tree.
Yes, we might have been loud.
Yes, it was disruptive in the hallway.
Yes, I will accept lunch detention.
Yes, let's just do it today and get it out of the way.
Yes, I'm wondering if Kate
is wondering
where I am.

• •

Alex	Alyx	Alexx
Starving.		
	Dehydrated.	
		Lost in a desert.
Wild eyes.		
	Desperate.	
		Searching, searching.
Our Redwood.		
	Our Ponytail.	
		An oasis in the hall.
Finds sustenance.		
	Quenches her thirst.	
		Eyes meet.
Catastrophe averted.		
	Breathes deep.	
		All is well again.

Kate

Hey, stranger,
my mouth says
before my brain even knows I'm talking.

I see you weren't abducted by aliens,
so,
whew.

Her head whips around,
she looks down
at me,
smiles
at me,
slams her locker
like an exclamation point.

Nah.
Had to fight off some giant
robots, though.

Well, I'm glad you survived.

Me, too.

Her smile is crooked,
the left side higher,
like it knows something the right side
doesn't.

Maybe we should walk to class
together?
In case the robots come back?

And you'll be my protector?

Um, of course.
I flex my arms.
She laughs.

I'll protect you all *the way to class.*

I think maybe the robots
are controlling me
because what am I even saying?

• •

TAM

Everyone says,
Hey, Tam! or
What's up, girl! or
Hey, nerd!
to me
as we walk by,
and I give out
all the
high fives.

Kate says hi
to everyone,
How's it going, Daniel? and
Hey, Sofie, and
I like that shirt, Grace,
as we walk by
and they all smile
like . . . I don't even know.

And it's so funny, right?
That she knows everyone,
and everyone knows me,
and somehow it took this long
for the two of us to meet?

• •

Kate	TAM
My mouth does the thing again, talking before I think,	
	She surprises me again, saying,
You're going to the game? *Right?*	
She makes a face like, Hello, crazy, Is there anything else to do on a Thursday night?	

I make a face, because
the Falcons were one game shy
of winning last year's
championship, so
duh
of course I'll be there,
everyone in town
will be there.

Fly, Falcons, fly!

I link my thumbs,
make my hands into wings.

Ever watched the cheerleaders?
During the game?

I have not once ever
even thought about
cheerleaders
while watching
a game.

Um. Maybe?

Whoa, whoa, whoa.
We're the best *part!*
And you don't watch?!
Well, now we can't be friends.

My eyebrows go sky high.

Her eyebrows go sky high.

I smile.
Just a joke.

She smiles.
What a turd.

Come sit by our bench,
watch me cheer . . .
and watch the game
if you have to.

Watch her cheer?
I start to laugh
because THAT
is the funniest thing
I've ever heard.
Watching flips and yells
instead of catches and runs?
Except.
I think about watching her
smile and cheer and clap
and yell,
I think about that ponytail
spinning like fireworks
and . . .

Okay. Fine.

And WHAT am I even saying?!
Okay?! Fine?!

I'll give it a go.
But I make no promises I'll—

Yay! Yes! You're going to love it.

Oh, will I?

You're going to.
I promise.

Promise, huh?

I smile.

She smiles.
I smile.

She smiles.

Whoa.

Whoa.

• •

TAM

Am I really going
to sit by the cheer bench?
With the moms
and the wannabes?
Instead of with the noisy crowd?
What if I get distracted?
Miss a sack?
Lose track
of the score?
But . . .

Kate asked me to.
Kate wants me to.
Ponytail was very
insistent,
and I guess . . .
what can it hurt?

I bet if I ask,
Levi will sit with me.
At least at first.

• •

Kate

Is she really coming
to the game?
Did I just ask-blurt that?
Why does it make me nervous?
Games don't make me nervous.
Nothing makes me nervous.
Except . . .
should I tell her I'll be hidden
under a giant falcon head?
Is she expecting to actually see, uh,
me?
Or does she even care?

And why
have I
just spent
ten minutes
worrying about this?
OMG.

• •

Kate

If you want,
you can meet me at my house
tonight,
and we'll go over
together.
I'll get you a good seat
so you can see the game
and, um,
me.
My mouth keeps talking
and I keep wondering
why I'm saying these things.
Bring someone with me?
When I should be focusing?
Prepping for the game?
Mom is going to freak.

• •

TAM

Okay.
Sure.
Cool.

And now I'm going to the game
with a cheerleader
and sitting behind the cheer bench
and
what
is
even
happening.
Robots must be
for real controlling me.

• •

TAM

Exactly five minutes
is how long I have
to shower
change
run to Kate's
so I can get a ride
to the game.

Why don't I
drive you to the game?

Mom shouts through
my closed door
but no
I don't want her to drive me.
I said yes to Kate
and I will go with Kate
and hopefully I won't be late
because argh
my hair
it looks so stupid
and this baggy shirt . . .
way extra dorky
and WHO AM I
worrying about these things?
Breathe, Tam.
Just brush your hair,
forget about the shirt,
and go.
Jeez.
It's only a football game.

Only a football game?!
Seriously.
Who
am
I
?

• •

Kate

Watching Mom is kind of fun
as she almost blows a gasket
looking at her watch
and at me
and the door to the garage
and back at her watch.
You'd think she
was the one
about to be late,
about to be yelled at.
She clears her throat.
I shrug.
I know Tam will be here.
I know she will.

The knock at the door,
a quick tap tap tap
reveals her,
out of breath
her smile big . . .
a little too big.

I laugh
and laugh
and laugh.

Hey.

Hey.

You made it.

I made it.

Your shirt's on
backwards.

Her eyes jump wide,
she looks down at her chest
starts to giggle.

Come on.
You can fix it in my room.

Mom looks at her watch.
Frowns.
Mom looks at Tam.
Frowns.
I march us
upward
out of here.

• •

TAM

A small bookshelf in her room,
perfectly made bed,
perfectly clean desk,
perfectly perfect
everything.

I take a book off the shelf.
It feels brand new.
The dust jacket slides
in my hand.

If you were a book,
what would your dust jacket say?

Her face, her eyes,
they both smile
as she tilts her head
to the side:

What do you mean?

Your story,
I say,
tapping the book.
How would I judge your cover?

Hmmm.

She twirls in a circle
once,
twice,
flops on the bed.

It would say:
Here lies Kate,
the smartest, most beautiful girl
who was the best at everything
but still a nice person
because that's important, too.

I laugh.
I think that was a
gravestone
not a dust jacket.

Close enough!
What would yours say?

Gravestone?
Or dust jacket?

Either.

Hmmm.

She sits up and watches me,
really stares,
dark eyes
sparkling.

Tam lives on a shelf
all her own.

We both laugh.

Girls! Hurry up!

• •

TAM

Book back on shelf,
I pull my arms into my shirt,
spinning it around,
sticking my arms out again.
Grinning faces accost me
from the wall behind her door.

You can't possibly like them.

Who?

MisDirection?
I point at the poster.
Maybe I pretend to gag.
A little.
The worst boy band of all time?

Shut up.

She throws a sock at me.

They're cute.
AND we're going to their show
for my birthday.
The whole squad.
We have an MDOMG countdown clock
and everything.

I pretend to throw up.
But I also laugh.
She throws her other sock.
I duck.

The music is catchy.

Catchy like the flu.
I walk over to the poster,
peer into all the eyes
peering back.

You know what?
They kind of look like girls.

They do not!

We both look at the poster
for a minute
then I throw the socks back at her
wham bam
and she laughs,
a sound I'm beginning
to want to hear
every second
of every day.

Girls! What's taking
so long?

• •

Kate

The look on her face
when I pull the giant falcon head
out of my closet
along with the wings
and the big
yellow
feet.
Hahahaha.

I put on the head,
bobble around.
Tam laughs and laughs
until Mom stands in the doorway
tapping her watch,
chewing her frown.

Let's get going, girls.
Katherine can't be late.

Mom continues to hate
the falcon head
but I don't want to fight about it
today.

• •

TAM

No one can see your pretty face
inside that thing.

That's what Kate's mom said to her
when she thought I wasn't listening.

You can't be captain of the squad
and a cartoon character
at the same time,
come on, sweetheart.

Her words came out pointed.
Sharp.
Stabbing darts.

Have some self-respect.
You don't want to be like Jill.
Let someone else be a goofball
so you can shine.

I heard it all
through the bathroom door
just before
I burst out,
caught Kate's eyes with mine.

What did my eyes say to her?
I'm not sure.
Maybe something like,
Yikes,
and
Who's Jill?

What did her eyes say to mine?
I'm not sure.
Maybe something like,
I'll tell you later,
and
Moms. Ugh.

• •

TAM

Tingling skull
just above my neck
the kind of feeling
that makes a kid sweat
like a whisper
a threat
a realization
a thought
a hit
to the brain,
thinking
maybe I shouldn't be here,
maybe I don't know Kate at all,
maybe her mom knows that, too,
I don't know
it's the way her mom looks at me
up and down
and down and up,
frown curling.
This place,
this house,
so clean,
so white,
I kind of
want to
run.

• •

Kate

Mom always smiles
when she says these things.
Telling me I'm beautiful.
Telling me I'm smart.
Telling me I'm not like Jill.
Telling me what I should be doing better.
Telling me what I'm doing wrong.
When she says these things,
I see Mom at her most smiley.

• •

Kate

I was so little when Jill left,
I can barely remember.
My big sister,
always yelling,
throwing things,
a tornado,
a siren.

She was the fly
in Mom's perfect soup.
She was the incessant dog barking
in Mom's quiet night.

And then she was gone.
A storm blown past.
Everything was perfect again.
Mom got her way.

They don't talk, of course,
so Mom hasn't heard
Jill is on her way home.
Well, not this home, but
this town,
and I'm so excited to see her;
it's been four years!
But she doesn't want me to tell Mom,
so I won't
even though . . .
wouldn't Mom want to know?

I'd hope so.

• •

TAM

The quiet lasts a little too long
before Kate's jaw
unclenches,
she smiles at me,
grabs my arm.

Let's get out of here!

We climb in the car
and as the seatbelts click, I watch:
her posture straightens,
her shoulders go back,
her chin sticks out,
she takes a deep breath.
She's like the Terminator
rebuilding herself.
I'm impressed how she does it,
quickly,
eyes facing front.
It makes me wonder how often
she rebuilds herself,
and if it's always
because of her mom.

• •

Alex	Alyx	Alexx
Well.		
	Well.	
		Well.
This mascot.		
	This falcon.	
		This Ponytail.
Will she have fire?		
	Will she have energy?	
		Will she have bounce?
She's had bounce.		
	She's had fire.	
		She's had energy.
All week.		
	At school.	
		And especially at lunch.

Kate

Dad always calls my
cheer uniform a costume
and Mom gets so mad,
because cheerleaders are
athletes, Fred.
Have some respect, Fred.
Would you say football players
wear costumes*, Fred?*

I wiggle my giant feathery fingers.
I stomp my enormous yellow feet on the turf.
Dad might win the argument for once,
if he wasn't away (*for work*).

(Though I have to say,
Dad's not wrong about my cheer uniform.
It does feel like a costume sometimes,
in a weird sort of way.
A costume of a different Kate.
A costume I wear every day.)

• •

TAM

My goober,
my shortstack,
my Levi is here.

Whew!
Things feel better now.
More normal.
Less weird.

I'm about to tell him
about Kate's mom
and how she's old
and kind of mean
and possibly
for some reason
hates me
but the band starts up,
everyone cheers,
the Falcons kick off,
and Kate . . .
hahaha!
Kate appears!

• •

Kate

I can't see that well.
I can't hear that well.
But it doesn't matter.
None of it matters.
I race around,
high-five the crowd,
I dance,
I goof,
I sweat,
I'm a mess.
And oh man, it's so much fun,
so
much
fun.
Because inside this thing?
I can be whoever I want to be.
Inside this thing?
I can scream
and no one can hear me.

• •

TAM

It's like she's magnified.
Her movements are hers
but so big.
She's come alive,
breathing life
into that ridiculous falcon head.
Bobbing
and goofing,
bouncing
and running,
egging on the crowd,
a full-on clown.
I can't believe it's her in there
but on the other hand
I totally can,
the more her face is hidden from sight
the more she's the Kate
I recognize.

• •

TAM

I tried to stay
to say
goodbye.
To glimpse
to catch
to earn
Kate's eye.
To whack her
Falcon shoulder
tell her
good job.
But her mom
came back
to pick her up,
her mom
waved me off,
said I'd better go
and now Timothy
—Levi's brother—
is giving us a ride home,
and everyone is quiet,
and I wish I could've stayed,
said bye to Kate,
watched that ponytail swing,
made her laugh
one last time
today.

• •

Kate		TAM
I can smile the smile		I smile the smile
act the act		I'm my own act
I can even trick myself		I am who I am
	inside	
for a little while,		most of the time
believe it		bona fide
	truth	
then I wonder		then I wonder
am I really the girl		am I really the girl
that everyone		the one everyone
wants me to be		*sees* as me
	deep	
	inside.	
Do people know		Is it possible
the dust jacket		my dust jacket
the story of me		this story of me
they read . . .		they read . . .
	is actually	
a story		a story
they write		they think
	about me	
instead of being		instead of being
the story that's actually		the story that's actually
	mine?	

• •

Alex

Our Ponytail.

Looks happy.

Our Redwood.

Looks exuberant.

Alyx

Our Falcon.

Seems excited.

Our Redwood.

Seems jazzed.

Alexx

Our cheerleader.

Distracted.

Our Redwood.

Demands focus.

TAM

Girl!
Girl!
Girl!
High-five!
I saw you flying
out on that field,
hilarious Falcon
egging on the crowd.
You were amazing,
crazy.
I was breathless just watching.
You looked like you were having
so
much
fun.
I take back
everything
I've ever thought
about cheerleaders
because . . .
Girl!
Girl!
Girl!
You are fierce
and strong
and whew!
I feel like
right here

right now
I should ask
for your autograph
cause you are . . .
For!
Real!

Kate stares at me,
her eyes a little wide
and oh good grief,
did I just sound like Mom,
biggest dork
on the planet?
Well.
I don't care.
It's all true.
Kate is for sure
for real
and I hope she knows it, too.

• •

Kate

I don't know what to say
to Tam's explosion of compliments
and shoulder punching
and excitement
when I know
I can't possibly be the mascot
anymore after this.

I have to give the job to someone else,
prep for captain,
lead the squad.

But her excited face
is kind of how I feel inside
if I can get Mom's voice in my head
to just be quiet.

It WAS really fun.
I DID do a great job.
I LOVED being goofy.
And the squad . . .
they moved and riffed
right along with me;
we were still a team,
they were all just fine.
In fact, everyone seemed
extra relaxed,
extra *good*, even,
without me barking orders
the whole time.

So what do I tell Mom?
What do I tell Coach?
I *like* being the Falcon.
I like it so much.

• •

TAM

She's quiet as I talk
which is weird
because she's usually
not.
So the words keep flying from my mouth,
unstoppable,
I don't know what else to do,
and Levi looks at me
like I've got some screws
loose,
but my mouth just runs
nonstop
and soon
Levi's huffed off
and I'm asking Kate
to come see *me* play,
to watch me spike and dive
and serve and win
and my chest puffs out,
my heart beating big
just thinking about her
watching me
from the stands.
I want to show off, too.
I want her to see me work, too.
I want her to know that I can sweat, too.
I want her to know how much I love what I do, too.

Her distant eyes
swerve toward me.
She blinks once
and after a pause
where maybe she wakes up
she smiles
and says,

Okay.
I'd love to see you play.

• •

Kate

Becca and the squad
eating lunch on the other side
of the cafeteria.

I should go over there
hang out
talk about
the game last night.

I should see who else
might want to be
the Falcon
next.

I should chat about Chloe's
MDOMG countdown clock,
see how many days left.

I should go now.
Over there.
Get up.
Walk over.

But Tam is talking about volleyball
and her eyes are so bright,
her smile so big.
She talks with her hands,
gestures wide,
knocking her milk over
twice
and I can't bear to leave her,
can't bear to go over there,
don't want to listen to Becca,
don't want to plot my takeover.
I like the Falcon.
I like lunch with Tam.

I wish
Mom's voice
would get out of my head.

• •

TAM

Shaking milk off my sleeve,
I laugh.
She does, too
and I ask:

Do you
want to come over
after school?

You could
go with us
to the match?

Watch me smash
the competition?

She laughs
again
and it makes me feel
light and bright.
I would do anything,
say anything
to hear her laugh
all night.

• •

Kate

Inside I feel a little zing
when I text Mom
about the volleyball game
and she says no
that I should come home
but I say I need to go
to check out the cheer squad,
the sixth graders,
the B team.
Maybe some of them will be good
and I can scout for next year's squad.
I hold my breath,
watch the
dot
dot
dots
Then . . .
it works!
My reward:

Fine. Yes. Okay.
But don't be too late.

I smile at Tam.
And I turn off my phone.

• •

TAM

This will be awesome.
This will be great.
Levi comes to nearly all of my games.
So it will be the same with Kate.
I won't be nervous
or act weird.
It's exactly the same, just . . .
there will be two friends
in the stands
cheering me on.
I won't feel nervous
or anything like that.
It'll be just a regular game,
no sweat.

• •

TAM

We walk quietly.

She bumps my arm.
I bump hers back.

We laugh.

Kate

We walk quietly.
I bump her arm.

She bumps mine back.

We laugh.

We pass Frankie's house.

An old lady is in her yard.

I wave.

She waves at us.

Hey, Frankie!

The old lady yells hello.
Another lady in the yard,
bent over a small pond,
stands,
holding a turtle,
smiles.

Hey, Roxy!

The other lady holds up the
turtle,
like she's about to say *Cheers!*

How's William?

Both ladies look up.
Both ladies look at the turtle.
Fine, they say,
in unison.

William waggles his feet.

The turtle waves hi, too.

You coming to my game tonight?

Sorry, William is busy,
the second lady says with a wink.

William waggles his feet harder.
I snort.
Does William know if YOU
are coming?

We'll see you there! they say,
still in unison,
making Tam laugh.

Kate watches us like she's never seen
two ladies, a kid, and a turtle
have a conversation before.

I've never seen two ladies, a kid,
and a turtle
have a conversation before.

Great! See you later, then.
We walk past them,
to my front door.

We walk past them to Tam's
front door.

This is going to be a great night.

Am I about to go watch
Tam's volleyball game with
two old ladies
(but not their turtle)?
That seems pretty . . .
exciting?

• •

Kate

Bookshelves smile
under the weight of so many books.
They curve and curl
looking soft
like a grandma's lap,
piled high
with all the best things.

Paths worn in the carpet
show years of feet
wandering to the kitchen
running to the bathroom
tip-toeing to the den.

And everything smells good.
Like love and books and
people and family.
Like dinner and plants
and cats
and
Tam.

The whole house hugs *me*
when I walk in.
Is that a silly thing to say?

• •

TAM

Mom.

Mom.

Stop.

Mom.

Mom.

Shhh.

No.

We just want a snack.

And to go to my room.

Mom.

Mom.

Stop.

Mom.

Mom.

Shhh.

MOM.

TMI.

MOM.

Well this was a terrible
terrible
idea.

• •

Kate

If I were standing under
a tree losing leaves
and those leaves flew down toward me
so fast
I couldn't catch
any of them
as they fluttered past,
and I tried to grasp
every single one
so I could inspect them,
look at their little leaf veins,
smell their outdoorsy scent,
memorize their color;
if I were standing under
that tree losing leaves
so fast
I couldn't catch
any of them,
it would be like right now
the rat-a-tat-a-tat
of Tam's mom
chatting about everything
all at once
and wanting to know *me*
more and more and more.

I want to catch all her words
all her questions
all the twinkles in her eyes,
hold it all in my hands
and breathe deep,
the newness of Tam
and her Mom
and her house
and her everything
seeping deep
into my soul.

• •

Kate

When Tam's mom asks
if I have any sisters or brothers
I don't even think before I say,

My sister Jill!
She's coming back to town!
I still can't believe
she was in the NAVY
all this time.
I haven't seen her in
so
so
long.

My voice trails off
as my brain catches up with my mouth,
as my eyes see Tam's mom smiling,
maybe a little surprised,
and Tam staring, like
WHAT, YOU HAVE A SISTER
WHO WAS IN THE NAVY,
WHAT.

She's a lot older than me.
My voice sounds stupid,
high-pitched now,
like I'm questioning what I'm saying.
She doesn't really get along with . . .
I . . .
Uh . . .
I . . . was a surprise baby.
Change of Life Child
or something dumb like that.
I . . .

Tam's mom puts her hand on my hand,
nods, her smile says *shhh*.
Then she tells me Tam should have a brother
but Tam ate him in her womb
and Tam screams

MOM! NO!

And everything is fine again.

• •

TAM

She said she'd make us snacks
but
she won't
stop
talking.

Mom.
OMG.
Mom.
Stop.

She's telling Kate everything
everything
about my life.
I did not *eat my brother*
in her womb,
good grief.
It's called Vanishing Twin Syndrome.
I looked it up a long time ago.
It happens all the time,
totally normal.

She's trying to be cool,
saying things like
amirite?!
and now she's asking more questions
about Kate's sister, Jill,

who I didn't even know existed
except for when Kate's mom
said she shouldn't be like Jill
and I was like
I wonder who that is
and
OMG.
Mom.
STOP.
STOP!

If I were Kate
I'd take a brownie
and run as far away
from this crazy woman
as possible.

• •

Kate

Her hair flies free
around her face,
wisps of gray
taking flight
like she's been mildly electrocuted.
And her smile is
full of light,
showing crooked teeth
that are lovely really,

imperfect
reality.
Tam's mom is a book
you can't judge by its cover
because she's wide open,
every page right there
to be read
in giant letters
begging you
to read more,
to flip through,
to lose yourself
in all her truths.

I can't help my eyes
as they grow wide
as Tam's mom goes
on
and
on
and
on.

I can't help but steal glances
at Tam
who looks ready
to explode.

• •

TAM

I know we have duct tape
in the junk drawer
behind
Mom's butt.
If I can get her to move
I can make a dive,
grab the tape,
and
seal
her
mouth
shut.
Shouldn't be too hard.
I think I can do it
and grab a brownie
to boot.

We should go to my room,
I say
my voice not as strong
as I want it to be.

Sorry to leave
you
alone,
Mom,
but as you always say,
you only YOLO once.

My eyes say
I am extra super
not
sorry.

We'll be ready to leave
pretty soon.
Cool?

Mom stares
into my face
and her lips twitch up
once
a move so tiny
only I would ever see it,
and the words she doesn't say
are louder than the words
she hasn't stopped saying.
Her eyes whisper,
When was the last time you had a friend over
who wasn't Levi?
They say,
A cheerleader?
They beg me,
I need to know more, more, more.

Twenty minutes.
Meet me in the car.
Leave the door open, you two!

I grab Kate's elbow
and half drag her
out of the kitchen
and to my room.
No duct tape necessary.
Today.

• •

Kate

I love
love
knowing
so many
new things
about her.

Is that weird?
I love seeing inside
her world.

I love
love
knowing
more
and
more

and
oooooof
she's dragging me
away.

• •

TAM

I shut my bedroom door
and lean against it
like we've just escaped
from a bear
or an axe murderer.

Kate laughs
and plops down onto my bed.

Your mom is . . .

I raise my eyebrows.

different than my mom.

Now it's my turn to laugh.

You think?

Kate shrugs.

Just a little.

And when she giggles
I see the brownie
stuck to her teeth
and it looks so sweet
and gross
my insides get warm
and melty,
a gross undercooked brownie
of their own.

• •

Kate

Her face crinkles.
Her eyes dip low.

Oh,

she says,

Yeah.
It's kind of a long story.

But I press
and ask
and cajole
and tease
and finally she tells me
how she lost a game,
punched a wall
and her mom found a frame
for the hole.

Her voice climbs high,
a cartoon voice
dripping with
goofiness,
punctuated with
pink cheeks:

Personal expression is art.
Feelings are for sharing.
A hole can be poetry.
Blah blah blah.

Tam flushes . . .
is she . . . ashamed?

My mom,

she says
with a shrug
eyes on the bare carpet,

is a hippie.
Can't you tell?

But I can only stare,
mouth open,
at the frame.

Worn carpet, sagging shelves,
and a hole in the wall?
My mother would burn this place down.
That's what makes *me* ashamed.

• •

Alex | Alyx | Alexx

Who do we have here?

Cheering at the game?

In an unofficial
capacity, of course.

Ponytail.

In the stands.

Smiling wide, wide,
wider.

Redwood.

Liquid fire.

As if no one else
is here.

But what about Levi?

Cooling off.

Watching close.

So much action.

On this Thursday.

At this volleyball game.

Kate

The two old ladies from earlier today
wave
from a few sections over
and Tam's mom waves back,
says,

I'm gonna run over there
and chat,
wanna come,
or are you okay?

But I can tell by her smile
she knows I'm going to stay
right here
in this seat
to watch the whole game.
And now,
by myself,
I allow a thing
I keep wanting to do:
I stare at Tam
as long and as hard
as I want to.
Everyone else in the stands
is watching too
so it isn't strange
for me to zoom zoom zoom
in
and memorize
the tall girl
my new friend

invading my thoughts
in a way so intense
it's like riding a wave,
climbing higher and higher.
The more I see her,
the more we talk,
the bigger the wave gets,
the more I feel . . .
swept up.

• •

Kate

She's so focused,
liquid and tall.
It's fun to watch her,
fun to watch the whole team,
but especially Tam.
And I actually like
that she hasn't found me
in the stands yet.
That way I can't mess her up—

Oh!

Hi!

Hi!

You're doing great!
Watch out!

Haha!

Oops.
She found me.
See?
She just missed the ball
because of me.

Extra oops.
See?
It makes me smile,
because she noticed me.

Sorry,
(not sorry)
rest of the team.

• •

TAM

It's just me and the ball,
the ball and me,
and the team
of course,
always the team.
But they know the ball and I,
we go way back,
best friends
connected
yin and yang.

The ball knows me
and I know the ball,
watching it fall
through the air,
connecting
leather
to skin:
BAM
over the net.
I am in the zone
until I hear a squeal,
a high-pitched cheer
that jolts
a lightning bolt
through my belly
and my eyes leave the court
and there she is
ponytail bright
under the lights
her squeal echoing in my ears
and I miss the point.

I miss the point!

The ball whizzes over my head,
just like that—
and what in the world just happened?
I don't *get* distracted.

• •

Kate

I want to describe how she moves
but I can't find the words.
It's like she knows where to go
before the ball knows where to go.
Her arms slice the air, so smooth,
finding the spot where the ball flies
and WHAM, whacking it sky high.
How?
How is she so quick?
Maybe she feels waves in the air,
ripples and trickles
caused by the flying ball.
Maybe she's a miracle of nature.
Her head whips around,
she catches my eye in the crowd
slams the ball
scores a point
finds me again
and winks.

• •

TAM

Mom
Frankie
Roxy
Levi
Kate
all waiting for me
after the game.
All smiling,
chatting,
congratulating,
but I just want them to go away.
Everyone except Kate.
Her cheeks are pink,
her ponytail bouncing,
I want to know more about
what she thinks,
if she had fun
tonight,
but Mom is chattering
and Levi is asking something
about joining chess club
and what
does that have to do with anything
right now
and we're all walking to the parking lot,
and I wish I was old enough
to have my own car.

• •

Kate

The lights are not very bright
in the parking lot.
Small halos fall,
little patches,
lighting up spots
next to a few of the cars.

Tam is bouncing,
energized,
talking about the game.
Her mom is being funny,
also bouncing,
also talking a lot.

A shadow breaks a halo,
two people by the car
next to us.
They are laughing,
quiet,
the sound carried low
on the night breeze
and I see
now they're kissing,
a quick peck on the lips.
Tam says:
Hey, Neighma!
Good night, sleep tight,
see you tomorrow!

And wait.
What?
Neighma is Frankie and . . .
Frankie and Roxy were
chicken-pecking
goodnight-kissing?
The two old ladies?
From this afternoon?
The halo of light
reveals a truth
I can't quite compute.
Tam's mom sighs.

I want to be that in love
when I'm their age,

Tam sighs back.

In love?
I ask, confused.

They've been married
my whole life,

Tam says,

even before
the Supreme Court
said they could.

And, huh.
Two old ladies
married to each other . . .
that isn't something
I've seen before.

• •

TAM

Kate runs to her front door,
waves goodbye,
disappears.

Mom's quietness
as she drives
burns my ears.
No more goofing.
No more jokes.
She pushes up her glasses
and finally she says:

Kate is nice.

Yes.

She seemed a little surprised
by Neighma and Roxy.

Yes.

Does it surprise you
that that surprises her?

I hadn't really thought about it.
I hadn't really thought about it.

And that's it.
No more words,
even once we get home.
Mom is never this quiet.
I guess maybe she's the one
who's surprised by
Kate being surprised.

But none of it surprises me.
I'm just glad
everyone was at the game
cheering me on.

• •

Kate

The call came late.
My eyes were closed;
I was already sliding into sleep,
tired from my day,
the game,
the newness of everything,
when the buzz on my dresser
startled me.
My heart jumped so fast and hard
it hurt in my chest.
What could Becca want this late?
Or maybe it's someone else?

Hello?

I didn't even look at the caller ID.

Katie?

My nose wrinkled.
Katie?
No one calls me that.

Sorry.
Wrong—

Katie.
It's Jill.

She tried to make me wait
until tomorrow
to see her,
but nope,
no way.

That phone call is why
I'm standing here
at 10:45 P.M.
in the dark,
my eyes scratchy,
hoping Mom doesn't notice
I'm gone.

The car door opens.
I climb inside.
There's so much trash on the floor
that when I kick it
it seems to kick back.
And then two long arms wrap around me.
I smell peppermint,
cigarettes,
the twang of hair gel.

Katie.

Her voice catches in my neck.

You're so big.

Jill.
My voice is quiet.
Maybe even scared.
You're so . . .
here.

She laughs, shows off
her lopsided smile,
hugs me tight.

• •

Kate

I don't know how to describe it,
the way Jill looks now,
like there's a light shining
from inside her,
little slants of sunshine
slipping around her smile.
She's bright,
happy,
relaxed.
Her eyes are a different shape
than they used to be,
not squinched,
not pinched,
but wide and smiling.

Smiling eyes?
Smiling eyes!
Jill.
Jill.
Jill.
I poke her
to make sure she's real.

• •

Kate

Four years ago.
The last time I saw my sister.
It was her eighteenth birthday
and she joined the Navy.
Mom yelled,
How could you do this to me?!
And,
The Navy?! You never even made it past guppies
in swim lessons, remember?
And,
But you're so pretty!
Why would you do that?!
And Dad,
he shut himself in his study,
while Jill hugged me hard,
her wet face sticking to my little cheek,
and she said,

I'm doing this for me, but also
for you.
I love you, Katie.
And then she was gone.
Four years ago.

• •

Kate

I don't want to stare.
I can't help but stare.
Her hair.
Dyed white.
Shaved on one side.
Flopping over her eye
on the other.

Her arms glow with colors,
designs
swirls
daggers
hearts
flowers.
I want to know the story
of every tattoo, and I can tell
from the way she smiles
she wants to tell me those stories, too.

• •

Alex | **Alyx** | **Alexx**

It's not just our eyes.

Seeing.

In the halls.

It's not just our ears.

Hearing.

At lunch.

It's everyone.

All over.

Everywhere.

Waking up.

Taking notice.

A constant hmmm.

A shift.

A tilt.

Something new.

Kate

I made you a thing.
(I really did.)
I don't . . . I don't know why.
(I really don't.)
But I just thought,
maybe you'd like it?
(I thought she'd like it.)
Though now that I'm looking at it,
it seems like maybe a thing
you would hate?
(She hates it.)
So . . .
never mind?
(I am such a dork.)
(I should walk away.)
(I am trapped here.)
(My eyes stuck to her face.)
(Her surprised face.)
(Her growing smile.)

Let me see it, you goof.

(This was a terrible idea.)
(What was I thinking?)

This is really cool.

You . . . like it?

I love it.
It's great!
Plus, the best part?

It was made by this girl,
she looks a little like a falcon,
Kate?
Have you heard of her?
Probably not.
She's very quiet and no one knows her,
she—

I laugh
punch her arm.

OW.
She punched my arm!

(Why would I do that?)
(Who AM I?)

Haha. No need to get violent.

(She likes it.)
(The bracelet, I mean.)
(Not the punch, probably.)
(Whew!)
(I can't stop smiling.)

(Look at her smile.)
(It makes me smile.)

(She's smiling, too.)
(I guess it was a good idea
after all.)

• •

TAM

Does it matter
that my heart races
in the halls at school?
Like,
maybe
I should see a doctor?
Because it's not cool
this crazy feeling
that's never happened before.

It doesn't happen
on the court
and that's when I work
the hardest.

It doesn't happen
when I'm almost late
and sprint super fast
to class.

It doesn't happen
when I talk to Levi
or when he makes me
laugh.

I don't get it.
These flutters
these heartbeat dives
into my toes
making my throat
close
and my breath
catch up high.

What's wrong with me?

And why does this happen only
when Kate walks by?

• •

Kate

We're standing in the hall
talking
laughing
as if we've known each other our whole lives.
I don't notice everyone disappearing.
I don't notice it getting quiet around us.
I don't notice the bell ringing.
I don't realize we're both late to practice.
Tam doesn't notice
either.

• •

TAM

Nothing makes me late to practice.
Nothing.
Not homework
or the dentist
or the weather
or detention.
Not Levi's jokes.
Not forgetting my stuff.
Not having a bad day.
Not anything.
Until today
when I was standing outside the gym
chatting with Kate
about her day
and we were laughing
and teasing
and talking
and then
like the shatter when you drop a glass
Coach Quick yelled

DaSilva!
What are you DOING out there?

and the lights seemed extra bright,
the sounds seemed extra loud,
like I'd just woken up
from a surprise nap
and oh crap!

Late!
Because of Kate!
Aaaack!

Coach!
Wait!
Let me explain!

• •

TAM

Shazam!
I knock over Levi's knight
and take out a few pawns,
too.
Oops.

What is that?

An extra secret chess move!

No, goob. On your wrist.

Do you like it?
A new bracelet.
I'm testing it out.

Bracelet?
What?
You're suddenly a girl or something?

Shut up.
I like it.

Who are you?
What did you do to Tam?

Shut UP.
It's cool.

I guess?
It just doesn't seem like . . .
you.

Like he's an expert
on me.
He takes my queen,
makes her dance,
just to rub it in.

But I'm distracted because . . .
isn't he an expert?
On me, I mean?
My best friend
shortstack
Levi twin?
Doesn't he know me
better than anyone?

IS this bracelet me?
Or is it the me
I want Kate to see?
Would I ever wear this normally?
What even IS normally
these days?
Yeah, it's ME, okay?!

Hey.

What?
It's ABSOLUTELY me!
The perfect me!
The exact me!
There has been nothing more ME
than this bracelet,
dude.

No . . . I just . . .
Jeez.
It's your move.

• •

TAM

I thought Mom might not notice.
I was wrong.

What is that totally radical thing
on your arm,
ma'am?

Nothing, Mom.
It's nothing.

It's not nothing!
Let me see that!
It's gooooooorgeous, Tam!
Super fly, tight,
am I right?

Mom.
Please.
Let go of my hand.

Did you buy this?
With what money?
Where?

It was a gift.

A gift?

Mom.
Stop.
No eyebrows.
Mom.

Her eyebrows have climbed
so high on her forehead
they are lost
among her bangs.

From whom, pray tell?

Just . . . a friend.

How do her eyebrows
get even higher?
Like caterpillars
escaping a fire.

Which friend?
The cute one?
With the ponytail?
Who came to the house?

Yes, Mom.
Kate.

Kate.

More eyebrows.

What?!

Kate?

It's no big deal!
Just a bracelet!

Okay!

Okay.

• •

TAM

Frankie stares.
I fume.
Why does Mom have to be so . . .
her?

. . .

Why can't she just be . . .
quiet?

. . .

Listen for once?

. . .

Not be so . . .
loud?

That's just who she is.

It stresses me out.

Why?

It just does.

. . .

Oh, come on, Frankie.
Don't look at me like that.

. . .

It just does!

Maybe you should think about
why her energy
stresses you out.
Is she saying something
you don't like?
Is she asking questions
you don't want to answer?

Now you're *stressing me out.*

Just something for you to think
about.
I like your bracelet, by the way.

ARRGHHHHHH.

What?

• •

TAM

Practice today.
But just before,
Kate sneaks away.
I do, too.
And we sit in the shade
surveying
the field,
the football players running around,
an airplane leaving a mark
across the sky.
It makes me sigh,
this quiet moment.
She doesn't need to talk.
I don't need to either.
We can just sit.
Side by side
and be . . .
together.

• •

Kate

We're too far away
for anyone to see
and I wish we could be
like this
all the time.

Our own spot.
Our own bubble.
It's so quiet,
so calm,
like we hit pause
and this moment is just . . .
our own.

• •

TAM		Kate
My sneaker.		Her sneaker.
Her falcon foot.		My falcon foot.
	Side by side.	
My elbow.		Her elbow.
Her elbow.		My elbow.
	Side by side.	
My hand.		Her hand.
Her hand.		My hand.
	Side by side.	
Leaning back,		Leaning back,
I feel the breeze.		The sun is warm.
The sun is warm.		I feel the breeze.
Everything		Everything
is quiet,		feels right,
feels right.		is quiet.
	Side by side.	

• •

TAM

There's a light in her eyes,
an ember
shining bright;
a tiny bit of heat
I always see,
always there,
and when I look too long
the ember
spreads the heat,
burns brighter
like a campfire,
a spark
electric arc
caught on a breeze.
Her ember eyes
take her burning light
making my own light
burn inside.

• •

Kate

What if we were walking to class?
What if my hand bumped hers?
What if my pinkie brushed her pinkie?
What if her pinkie caught mine?

What if they linked together?
What if they swung back and forth?
What do you think would happen?
Would anyone see and laugh?
Would we both pretend it didn't happen?
Would my heart threaten to explode?
Would the world end?

• •

TAM

Her pinkie bumped my pinkie
as we walked to class.
Then it bumped again,
a little sideswipe,
a little grin.

And then once more,
a pinkie tap,
a little Morse code,
saying hello.

Then a third time,
a gentle crash;
but this time
my pinkie curled,
it clasped,
making a grab,
making a catch,

a trapeze artist
mid-air grasp,
and her pinkie clasped too,
and they caught together,
swinging,
monkey tails
in the zoo.
Tangled-up pinkies
curled up together,
swinging,
clinging,
knowing exactly what to do.

• •

Kate

What does holding hands even mean?
Maybe your hand is cold.
Maybe you're lost.
Maybe it's a game.
It could be anything.
I hold Dad's hand.
(Well, not really anymore.
He's gone all the time.)
I hold Mom's hand.
(Well, not really anymore.
I'm too old.)

I could hold anyone's hand
if I wanted to,
but only if anyone's hand was Tam's hand
because that's the *only* one I want to.

• •

TAM

Energy force
invisible torch,
heating up the skin on my arm.

Her elbow buzzing close,
whispering hello
to my own elbow
without touching,
but somehow doing
so much more.

And Levi is talking,
saying something about class
but I can't hear him,
the buzzing is too loud
elbow to elbow
I can only look down,
eyes fused
melted to
her arm
looking soft in the light.

And there's a tilt in the world
as the buzz of her arm
connects with my arm
and my face flashes hot
and my eyes shoot up
and I wonder if the whole lunchroom just heard
the zippity zap pop
of electricity
that came from her.

• •

Kate

Here's the thing.
I am not a baby elephant.
I have never actually seen a baby elephant
in real life.
But I've watched videos.
Tons and tons of videos.
And a baby elephant does this thing
where it runs around to explore.
Then every few minutes
it runs back to its mom
and touches her trunk
or snuggles her leg
and then it runs off again
like its mom has given it energy,
like it can last a few more minutes
in the big

huge
gigantic world
because it just touched home
for a second.

Like I said,
I am not a baby elephant.
But when I see Tam in the halls,
or in the lunchroom,
and her eyes catch mine . . .
I feel like,
for the next few minutes,
the big
huge
gigantic world
is safe,
it's mine.

• •

TAM

I see her over there:
Kate's friend,
Becca.
She points her yearbook camera at us.
The shutter
snaps
snaps
snaps

like exclamation points
hurled through the air.

After a minute,
the snaps stop.
The camera drops.
She watches us
blink
blink
blink
before she turns
and walks away.

Becca, with her perfect hair,
Becca, usually so chatty,
instead
stays quiet,
eyes drop to the floor
as she rounds the corner
and I wonder
what
what
what
is going on
in that shiny head of hers.

• •

Alex	Alyx	Alexx
What's cookin'?		
	Brownies, cakes, sweet treats!	
		Oh my!
Oh my!		
	Who's cookin'?	
		Cheer squad!
Bake sale?		
	Bake sale!	
		Bake sale!!!
But wait . . .		
	But wait . . .	
		But wait . . .
Is that . . .		
	A helper?	
		Oooh.
Sweet intrigue . . .		
	Surprise!	
		Extra treat?

TAM

You want me to bake *today?*

Kate

Oh, come on, silly,
it's not that hard.
You mix eggs and sugar and flour
and ta da
you have a cake
or cookies
or whatever you want.

TAM

You are not familiar
with the destruction
of Birthday Cake '17.
You have not heard of the
Infamous Exploding Ham Incident
of '15,
have you?

Kate

We could find marshmallows
and butter
and Rice Krispies
and make a bunch of treats.
Those don't explode
unless you count
the snap crackle and pop
in your mouth
when the goo
hits your tongue.

I'm telling you,
me in a kitchen
is a recipe
for disaster,
my friend.

Come on, silly,
help me out.
The big bake sale needs us.
Plus, it'll be fun.

Fun?
Sure.
There's nothing more fun
than a house burning down!

• •

Kate

I'm bringing Tam home
to help
with the bake sale,
my fingers type out
on my phone
until
they do a thing on their own,
tapping the backspace
erasing
the words.

Mom probably won't be there;
it's wine club night.
So does it even matter
anyway
if I say
who's coming home with me
from school?

When Becca comes over
I never tell Mom,
so why would I tell her
with Tam?

I slide my phone back in my bag.
I wave my pinkie at Tam.
My stomach does a little leap,
like I'm being sneaky
or bad.

(But that's crazy, right?
Why would Mom have a problem with this?
We're baking for the squad.)

• •

TAM

A museum
of The Perfect Life
with plenty of
Perfectly New Furniture and
Perfectly Clean Bedrooms.

A house where you
take off your shoes,
leave them neatly by the door,
where there's a living room
no one goes in
and a dining room
just for show.

Your house is like a magazine,
I say,
kicking off my shoes.

Nah.

She straightens our shoes,
lines them up,
soldiers at the door.

You should see upstairs.
The remodel just started.
There are holes in the wall!
Like yours.

Like mine?
Her face turns pink,
she looks at the floor,

I mean, like in your room.
The hole you punched.
Uh.
I guess it's not really like that at all.

I watch her for a second,
shifting from foot to foot,
turning pinker and pinker,
then I laugh,
I guess your remodel guys
really want to win at volleyball, too.
She smiles,
back to her regular self.

Something like that.
Come on.
Let's conquer the kitchen.

Oh, girl,
be careful what you wish for.

• •

TAM

Oh!
Shazam!
Look what's not here!

Two eggs?
Nope?
Looks like they've disappeared.
Looks like we're gonna have to
pop by the store
and grab
some already-made stuff.
Looks like you've been saved
from my exploding history
from my giant puffs
of stinky smoke
that tell the whole neighborhood
oh hey look
Tam is once again
attempting to cook.

• •

Kate

I can't help but laugh at Tam,
so dramatic,
so not wanting to cook.
Ten feet tall in the kitchen,
able to reach any cabinet
in a single bound,
but missing the fact
that
the eggs

are right in front of her
on the counter
because I'd already pulled them out.

• •

TAM

A poof.
A cloud.
A laugh.
She looks up from the bowl,
her eyebrows
powdered,
a revolutionary wig of
momentary confusion.
She sputters,
flour puffs from her lips.
I laugh again.

Not all at ONCE, Tam!

She laughs,
throws a pinch of flour,
flicks it
at my own brows.

Half-cups at a time, dummy!

Who are you calling dummy?
I throw a pinch of flour back,
and then
more poofs

more clouds
more laughs
more poofs
more clouds
more laughs.

A thought hits me
just like a poof of flour
exploding in my mind:
How is it that Kate makes me like
all the things I never have before?
Bracelets,
cooking,
and—

Girls!
Enough!

Uh-oh.
Kate's mom.
Lips in a line,
cardboard box in her arms,
wine bottles peeking
at us.
Flour dust
catches in the air
in the light
like
it has frozen
with us.

• •

TAM

I hear them
in the other room,
hushed whispers
that are somehow
also loud.
Something about

You didn't think to ask?

and

Is this really the best friend
for you?

• •

TAM

I want to explain.
My mom and I . . .
we have food fights all the time.
It's messy and gross
and dumb and funny
and I just thought everyone . . .

But I can't find the words, exactly,
and Kate's mom stares at me
like she's mad at me
for things I don't even know about,

and maybe she has
some kind of special kitchen
that gets ruined if it's messy.
I don't know
though,
that would be a dumb
design.

If I could just find the words
maybe Kate wouldn't be in trouble.
Maybe I could save her.
But everything sticks in my throat
just like the flour stuck in my hair
and none of my words shake loose
like the flour I'm dripping everywhere.

• •

Kate

She *would have* expected more.
She *would have* expected better.
She *would have* been less disappointed with
less
mess.

Not very *ladylike*,
this
mess.

Not very *ladylike*,
at
all.

Well what if I'm messy sometimes?
What if my *ladylike*
has a different definition than hers?

• •

TAM

Kate comes back to the kitchen,
ponytail wonky,
still covered in flour.
Her eyes stare at the floor.

It's about to be ripped up, anyway.
Why does it matter if it gets dirty?

Katherine.

Her mom's voice is a low growl.

Kate's eyes meet mine.
In a split second
I see them flash,
saying so many words
I can barely keep up.
But her mouth just says,

I'll walk you to the door.

Her floury elbow catches mine
and she spins me out of the kitchen,
chin high.

• •

TAM

William looks up at me,
raises his turtle claw in
slow-slow-slow motion.
I raise my hand in
slow-slow-slow motion.
We slow-slow-slow high-five.

I clear my throat.
Frankie's side-eye
appraises.

Is my chest burning
from Frankie's very hot,
very spicy
Mexican hot chocolate?
Or is it burning because Kate's mom
hates me
for no real reason?
(Not counting the kitchen mess.)

Something on your mind?

William blinks.
I blink.
Are you kidding me?
Was that a *tear?*
Am I *crying*?
Ugh.
Why would I cry?
I never cry.

Do you mind my asking,
what is in your hair?

I look up,
put my hand in my hair.
A tiny explosion of flour
falls on my lap,
falls on William,
and just like that,
it reminds me of Kate.
It makes me smile.

The burn in my chest gets warmer,
brighter, as I tell Frankie the story,
and we laugh together.

• •

Kate

I don't feel like talking to Mom
anymore
today.
And I can tell she doesn't feel like
talking to me
either.

But my brain is moving in circles,
overlapping,
spinning,
there are so many thoughts
going so many ways
sparks might shoot out of my ears
like those firework daisy chain things.

I want to write it out,
or talk to someone,
but I don't even know what
I want to say.
I just feel kind of crazy
and
hey,
I know . . .

Hey,
I text Jill.
What's going on?

• •

Kate

The saw is so loud
I can feel it in my teeth,
vibrating,
screaming,
a banshee.

Mom waves her hands, frantic,
telling me to move.

Don't stand there!

Her mouth moves.

No weight!
Move! Move!

I look down.
Part of the floor,
new,
gray,
wide wooden slats.
An empty color.
But pretty, I guess.
I step to the side.
Mom mouths,

Thank you.

I'm going to see Jill tonight,
I say,
knowing the saw is drowning me out.

Pardon?

She cups her hand
around her ear.

Have you missed her?

She shakes her head.

I can't hear you!

What else is new?
I shout back,
maybe a little too loud.

• •

TAM

Mom calls me homegirl while
the pancakes sizzle
and she wants to know about my day
and she had a million patients
and she's so tired.

I've already showered
the flour
away
and I'm also so tired
so I just
say,
My day was fine,
and we eat our pancakes
in silence.

• •

Kate

I told Mom I have a group project,
imperative to study
at the library,
nowhere else,
only the library
will work.
As soon as Mom dropped me off
Jill drove up,
whisking me away,
asking about my day.
And the funny thing is,
now that I have the chance to talk,
to let the daisy chain sparks fly,
to figure out my spinning brain,
I only want to talk about Tam
and how she looked in the kitchen,
all powdered and messy,
and how much I *liked* to see her
in my kitchen
instead of in school
or on the volleyball court.
She was right there,
and I was right there,
and no one else was
right there,
and it was

so
much
fun.

But all these words spark in my head
and can't quite find their way
to my voice
so I say,
My day was weird, but good.
How was yours?

• •

Kate

Jill is quiet, then
she talks about looking for a job,
and other things.
I don't really hear her because I'm
staring into her black coffee eyes
reflecting my face
and I wonder if her face reflects in my eyes
and how it is that
the two of us
are created from the same ingredients
when she seems so black coffee deep
and I am so
milkshake messy.

Her eyes stare back,
holding my gaze,
and I wonder . . .
is she looking for herself in me?

• •

Kate

Jill's eyes move to the window,
a slow slide,
when I ask if she's going to come home,
to see Mom.
She spins her spoon in her coffee
as she sighs and shrugs.

I feel that sigh.
I feel that shrug.

The floors are all ripped up,
and Mom seems fresh out of hugs.
Maybe it's not a great time to visit
right now.

• •

Alex	Alyx	Alexx
Alyx?	Alexx?	Alex?
Do you feel	Do you feel	Do you feel
extra feelings	extra feelings	extra feelings
today?	today?	today?
I don't.	Not me.	Definitely not.
But everyone else?	But all the people?	But the lunch tables?
Might be a revolt.	It's tense out there.	So many feelings.
In the air.	In the air.	In the air.

Kate

I guess Becca called
the house phone
when I was with Jill
yesterday.
No one calls the house phone.
Mom thought I had died or something.
An emergency.
But it was because Becca wanted to say hi
and she thought maybe my cell phone was broken
or taken away
because I haven't been answering her calls
or texts.
That hasn't been on purpose,
I swear.
I've just been busy,
distracted,
and I see her at practice every day!
But Mom was freaked
and she wanted to know why.
Why, Katherine,
why haven't you been talking to Becca?
Are you fighting?
She's an ally, *you know.*
You need her on your side
when it's time to take up the reins
of captain.
Maybe take a minute tomorrow.

Sit with her,
see how she's doing.
She's your best friend,
why would you ignore her?

I'm not ignoring her,
I just . . .
I don't know.
She's not who I want
to talk to
right now.

But here I go . . .
a diplomat.
a leader.
a captain.

• •

Kate

Hey, Becca.

Hey, Kate.

What is that?

A pomegranate.
Want some?

Sure.

You like it?

It's tart.

Like you.

Like me?

Looks sweet, but
complicated on the inside.

Am I complicated?

Tam walks by, all swagger
and laughing.
The room tilts toward her,
orbiting her.
She is the bright star
in the center of the lunchroom universe
and I am in a pomegranate black hole
watching Becca stare at her fruit,
concentrating so hard
to pick out the tiny bites.

Did you bring something?
For the bake sale?

No I didn't.
I forgot.

Oh, huh.
Hey, Kate?

Yeah?

Yearbook!

She surprises me
flash flash flash.
I don't have time
to smile.

• •

TAM

I see Kate
leaning close to Becca
far away
heads bent
secrets shared?
I want to hear every word.
I want to memorize every detail
of what's on Ponytail's mind
today,
and I want that Becca girl
to melt
melt
melt
away
but she doesn't, so I look around,
I see my man's man
ladies' man
man about town
waving
wearing
a protein shake mustache
like he's king of the world
and I laugh.
My shortstack
Levi
best bud

sitting tight
holding court
with the other goofballs
at lunch.
I drop my tray
WHACK
on the table,
straddle the bench,
high-five low-five
fake punch
smile
and just as Levi starts to chat
I stop listening
because finally,
finally,
Kate
is heading this way.

• •

Kate	TAM
She's not that bad.	
	[side-eye]
Tam. *It's true.*	
	[side-eye] *Your mom hates me.*
She does not!	
	[side-eye]
Well, I mean *she hates* *everything.* *Not exclusively you.*	
	[side-eye]
I'm sorry. *When you said you'd blow up the kitchen,* *I didn't think you were serious.*	
	[shoulder punch] *Next time, believe me.* *I'd never lie to you.*
Deal. [smile]	
	[smile] *Your mom still scares me.*
I know. *She scares me, too.*	

• •

TAM

I look around after school
(but maybe not too hard)
and I don't see Levi.

I meant to ask him
(but maybe wanted him to say no)
if he's going to tonight's football game.

I don't see him
(because I've stopped looking)
so that means I'll go alone.

Maybe I'll sit by the cheer bench
so I can see what the mascot is up to.
(It feels important to know.)

• •

Kate

I guess this is it.
Our last game together.

The Falcon's eyes are empty.

I admit,
I won't miss your smell.
But we did have fun,
didn't we?

The Falcon's beak is still.

Thank you for not caring
if I was dumb
or dorky
or silly
or clumsy.

The Falcon's feathers ruffle
in the breeze.

Thank you for hiding me,
but also not hiding me,
if that makes any sense
at all.

I hate to give you back.
I hate to be done.
We had a good time, didn't we?
You goofy Falcon.

I put on the Falcon head,
take a deep breath.
Tonight after the game
I'll give Coach the costume back.

Time to listen to Mom.
Time to focus on captain.

• •

TAM

Rumbling stumbling tumbling chaos
another mascot at the game?!
Kate didn't say anything about—
Whoa, whoa!
Hahahaha!
The coaches run and yell,
chasing the new mascot
right off the field.
It must've
just been
some kid
goofing around.
Oh man,
oh wait,
Kate.
She isn't laughing.
Not even close.
Falcon head under her arm,
girl is breathing fire.
Who was that masked chicken?
She looks ready to take its head off
in more ways than one.

• •

Kate

Rogue!
Imposter!
Fake!
Jerk!
Did you see that guy?!
Some kid trying to steal my spotlight?!
Some kid trying to make me look dumb?!

You didn't look dumb at all.
I promise.
It was just some dopey kid.
No big deal.
You were great.
Just like you always are.

Tam met me after the game,
after the squad went on and on and on
about that stupid chicken head,
how funny he was.
And now I'm squeezing the Falcon,
the giant head pressed to my chest,
and Tam is talking,
but I can't hear anything she says.

I *know* I looked dumb.
Even through the giant head
I could hear all the laughs.
AHHHH.
My brain is red.
On fire.

Flames.
Shooting from my eyes.
I'M the mascot.
Tonight was MY night.
My LAST night.
Why would someone try to steal that?
Well guess what?
They can't have it.

What?

They can't have it.
I'm not going to quit.

You were going to quit?

Tonight was my last night.
No more Falcon.
Back to the squad full-time.

But why?
You love the Falcon.
You can't do that and *be captain?*

I don't want to explain it.
I don't want to talk anymore.
I want to find that chicken head
and rip him apart
feather by stupid feather.

The Falcon is *me*.
And I am it.
We are the same.
The squad and Mom . . .
well, they'll just have to deal with it.

• •

Alex

Everyone is talking.

That fake mascot.

That poor Ponytail.

Wondering.

Alyx

Everyone is talking.

Running amok.

Eyes ablaze.

Wondering.

Alexx

Everyone is talking.

Ruckus.

A scandal.

Who is stealing
her show?

TAM

I've never seen her like this,
sullen,
quiet.
No smile,
not even when Becca yells,

Yearbook!

for the 47,000th time,
snapping pictures
like it's an emergency.

I poke her shoulder,
steal her chips,
but nothing works.
The bell rings so I grab my tray,
follow Levi
who is extra energetic today.

See you later, Kate,
but she doesn't even wave,
just looks up for a second
before she walks away.

• •

Kate

Fine.
Whatever.
Everyone is talking about the rogue.
The fake.
The other mascot at the game.

Fine.
Whatever.
Everyone thinks it was funny.
But didn't they see *me*?
How hard *I* worked?
How my routine was choreographed?
Practiced?
Perfect?

Fine.
Whatever.
Like I care *at all*.
Next game I'll be so good,
and that turd will be forgotten.

• •

TAM

Volleyball juggernauts,
speeding comets
destroying everything,
leaving craters
in their wake.

I smash them in the backyard,
pounding,
one by one
even though
we're supposed to
save our energy
for the game.

But I have too much energy,
too much . . . something.
Kate barely talked to me today,
and I don't know what that means.

• •

Kate

Obviously, Mom does not know
about the rogue,
the imposter.

Obviously, Mom thinks
I've already quit
the mascot.

Obviously, I'm going to
have to tell her
that the Falcon is still alive,
wings beating.

But first,
obviously,
I need to practice more,
get better
so I can smash that imposter
and be the best.

• •

TAM

Like three words.
All day.
That's it.

I twist the bracelet,
her bracelet,
around and around
my wrist.

. . .

Frankie.
Neighma.
Come on!

Three words all day?
That can be a lot
as if they're important words.

Argh!
Frankie!
You are not Yoda!
Help me!

Frankie refills my steaming tea.
She does the thing
where she tries to hide her smile
by looking in the corner
of the room instead of
at me.

Meercat climbs my arm.

Just because she feels bad in general
doesn't mean she feels bad
toward you
or because of you.
Let her feel her feelings.
That's the nicest thing you can do.

Should I see if she wants to come tonight?

Neighma puts her hand on my shoulder,
squeezes,
takes Meercat.

Let her be.

But . . .

She'll feel the feelings.
Then she'll be all right.

You give terrible advice.

Frankie squeezes my shoulder again.

No I don't.

• •

Kate

Jill's sofa is so lumpy
like little gnomes
live inside
poking your butt
while they giggle and hide.

I tell her about the mascot imposter,
out of nowhere,
stealing the show,
making me look dumb,
and how super unfun
that was.

I tell her how I need to tell Mom
I can't be captain anymore.
I need to use all my energy
to get that imposter
off the field.
I'M the mascot.

(Even if it's still technically temporary.)
It's MY job.
(Even if it's supposed to be
for only a few games.)
I like it.
I'm good at it.

And then it hits me
lightning to the skull:
Being the mascot is *more fun than cheering*.

Whoa.

Maybe the fake mascot
will be at Tam's game
and I can brain him with a volleyball.

Come on! Jill! Let's go!
It'll be fun.
You can watch Tam
in all her glory.
Or, just, you know,
maybe you can meet her,
and I can kill a chicken.
We can make it just in time!

• •

Kate

Well, finding the chicken was a bust,
no such luck
tonight.
But Tam is on fire,
making me forget
just how mad I still am.

Is it weird that I didn't tell Tam
I'd be at the game tonight?
I want Jill to meet her
without meeting her,
to see her,
a stranger,
lighting up the night.

• •

TAM

It's time for me to
throw
down
show
down
slam
dive
win

but when
I look out in the crowd
to fill up on the cheers
I see Kate!
Hey!
But . . . she's laughing
with another girl
way older
way not our age
and the girl puts her arm around Kate
and the ball sails over my head
snapping
cracking
in the corner of the court
a point
for the other team
and my head feels like the ball
smacked into IT
because
uh
who is that girl with Kate?

• •

Kate

If I could snap my fingers right now
and freeze everyone in the building
except for myself
I would do it.
SNAP.

Then I'd push through all the frozen people
gently
quietly
so I could stand right next to Tam,
arm in the air
waiting for the ball.
I would walk up to her,
walk around her,
look at her long legs
so muscle-y.
Look at her face,
so concentrate-y.
I would stare in her eyes,
memorize their flecks
of black and brown
and gray.
I would maybe push a curl
out of her face,
tuck it back under her headband.
I might leave my hand on her face
for just a second,
to feel how warm her cheeks can be,
and then I'd go back
back
back.
SNAP.
And no one would know
I'd left my seat.

• •

TAM

I waited for her.
For them.
After the game.
I wanted to show her
I wore the bracelet she made
for good luck,
and it worked!
We won anyway,
despite me missing three points
THREE POINTS
and not getting my head in the game.
I waited for her.
For them.
After the game.
But they didn't stay.
They disappeared.
And I didn't get to find out
who that was with Kate.
I didn't find out
that other girl's name.

• •

Kate

Can we stop for a milkshake, Jill?
Before I go home?

Sure, kiddo.

Can you tell me about where you've been?
For so long?

Sure, kiddo.

Can you tell me why you're back?
And what your plans are?

Sure, kiddo.
Maybe I could ask you
some questions, too?
If I can get a word in?

Sure, kiddo.

• •

Kate

Ships as big as cities,
traveling all over the world,
hard work,
good friends,
training.
Jill tells me about the past four years
as I drink my milkshake.
I know I was the one who asked her.
But I can't concentrate.
All I keep thinking about is,
if I really could freeze everyone,
have Tam all to myself,
what would that mean?
How would I feel?

Our pinkies catch,
the words come out before I can think,
interrupting Jill.

Hmm? What?

Grasp by grasp.
We never talk about it.
We never say,
hey,
are we holding hands?
or, What is happening?
but it's always the same.
Her pinkie finds mine,
or mine finds hers
whenever we walk sigh by sigh
I mean

my cheeks burn

side by side.

• •

Kate

You and Tam, you mean?

My heart pounds.
What am I doing?
What am I saying?
I stare so hard at my milkshake,
I think the glass might shatter.

Yes.

Does it bother you?
That you hold hands?
Or does it bother you
that you never talk about it?

Both?

I still can't look up.
My hands are frozen on my milkshake,
but I can't let go.
My traitorous hands.
My deviant pinkies.

I'm guessing
just guessing . . .
you haven't talked to Mom?
About this?

My laugh is a short burst,
a throat fart.

What do you think?
Especially after the
flour fiasco,
especially if I really want to
quit trying to be captain.
WWMT, Jill?
What
Would
Mom
Think?

Maybe she'll surprise you.

She'll say I'm distracted,
I need a better friend,
she'll ask about Becca . . .
ugh.

Maybe just try *talking to her.*

I'd like to point out
this is pretty bold advice
from someone who joined the Navy
to avoid talking to Mom,
but I don't.

• •

TAM

It's probably too late,
but I'm going to do it anyway.
I sneak down the hall,
in the dark
to the kitchen
to find my phone
that Mom confiscates at night.
If she catches me
she'll be
so bummed, Tam,
just really bummed.
Phones steal your soul,
and nighttime is for
replenishing your soul.
Blah blah blah.

Are you awake?
I text.
My heart pounds
as I slide to the kitchen floor,
hiding.

Sorry it's so late.
I text.

I wait.
Nothing.
It's probably too late.
Then!
dot dot dot

Hi

Hi
I saw you at the game tonight

You were great!
(as usual)

I totally was not.
I got distracted.
I
I think about my next words.
What exactly to say.
Maybe just . . .

Oh yeah btw,
who was that girl with you?

That's my sister, Jill!
I thought she'd like to see a game.

Her sister!
Of course!
My head knocks back
against the countertop,
my neck suddenly loose
with relief.
I didn't even know it was tied up in knots
until it wasn't anymore.
Ouch.

Oh! Cool,
I text.
You should've said Hi.

I know. I'm sorry.
We had to run.
I definitely will next time.
☺

I stare at the smiley face,
burn it into my brain.
There's so much more
I'd like to ask
but to do that,
I have to be alive
and I won't be
if Mom catches me
so I write . . .

Well, anyway.
I just wanted to say Hi.
And goodbye.☺

Hi and goodbye! ☺

Good night, Kate.

I rub my head where I bonked it,
and I take a deep breath—
maybe the first deep breath I've taken
all night.

• •

Kate

Mom was embarrassed when Coach called
to apologize about the rogue mascot,
to say how well I've been doing,
how the squad is pleased
I've decided to be the Falcon
for a little while longer.

Mom thinks we should:
call Coach back
set up a meeting
discuss my cheering
and put this *Falcon thing*
behind us.

Because you love cheering,
Katherine.
You always have.
Don't settle for being regular
when you know you can be better.

• •

Kate

I look at the torn-up floor,
the living room reborn.
I feel like, inside,
my guts are the same.
I'm breaking apart,
changing,
and it's happening faster
every day.

I mean, Mom's right.
I *do* love cheering.
It's a constant.
A bond.

Mom was cheer captain
when she was my age,
then a legend through college, and
she always says
this is her gift to me:

my athletic ability,
my leadership,
my cheering.

I don't know.
Maybe she's right.
I've worked hard to be captain,
to be on the right track.
It's super dumb to quit all of that
just to fight with a chicken.

Except. Except.
Who *am* I right now?
I mean, really?
Mom thinks she knows,
but how *can* she if I don't?

I look at the floor.
Yep, just like my guts.
Torn to bits.
A mess of shreds.
I should listen to Mom, right?
She always knows best.

And yet . . .
my torn-up guts are whispering to me,
calling my name.
I can tell it's something big,

something important
I just can't quite understand
what they're trying to say.

• •

TAM

Kate breezes by,
waves,
heads to her locker.
Becca yells,

Yearbook!

And flash, flash
she's like Kate's own personal
paparazzi.

It makes me think
that last year,
if I'd seen this little scene,
Levi and I
would have made so many jokes.

But now . . .
I watch from over here
and it's all in slo-mo
and my heart pounds this crooked beat
as I think:
If you lived your whole life
never feeling your heartbeat
you wouldn't miss it, right?

You'd just do homework
watch TV
sleep
and that would be that.
You can't miss something you don't know.

But then
what if one day
you woke up and
ba-bump, ba-bump, ba-bump
there it was?
You'd maybe grab your chest in surprise:
ba-bump ba-bump ba-bump
ba-bump ba-bump ba-bump.
Your heartbeat would get faster,
your eyes might go wide,
and finally, finally
you'd know what it feels like
to be alive inside.

This is how I feel every day.
Every day.
When Kate walks by.

Yearbook!

Becca yells
and I smile
at the flash flash flash
matching my heartbeat
that was missing
until now.

• •

Kate

Black splotches in my eyes
from Becca's camera
make me blink
and as I blink
I see a sign
taped to the wall.
Student council elections
coming up soon.

And.
Hmm.

THAT's an idea.
If I decide to stay being the mascot . . .
if Coach is cool with that . . .
and *if* I give up the captain plan,
Mom will be totally mad.

But.
But.

If I do something more . . .
do something better . . .
I can show Mom.
I can go even bigger.

What if I run for class president?
Student Council won't know what hit them.

Mascot and president.
Best of both worlds.
Mom will see the truth.
I'm better than normal.
More than regular.
I'm queen of the school.

• •

TAM

Hello, little pinkie.
How are you today?
Have you missed me
since yesterday?

My voice is high-pitched,
silly,
like a Muppet
talking quietly
out of the side of my mouth.

Kate looks up at me,
even with her head pointed down.
She wiggles her pinkie
before she curls it around
mine and says
in her own Muppet voice,

I had little pinkie dreams
all last night
about finding you today
and holding you tight.

We are such huge dorks.
Big, giant goobers
as we burst out laughing,
swinging arms in the hall
and Muppet-ing our way to class
in our own goofy bubble.

• •

Kate

You'll get us in trouble.

TAM

For passing notes?
No one cares.
Tell me more about Jill.

She's my sister.

Duh.
And she's in the Navy.

Was in the Navy.
She's out now.
Back home.
Well, not home home.
But here.
In town.

Why not home home?

Long story.

We have 53 minutes of geography left.

Ha.

Really, though.
Why not home?

She and Mom don't get along.
Mom thought Jill should go to college.
Jill wanted to see the world.
Mom thought Jill had bigger potential.
All they did was fight.
So Jill left.
And it's been four years.
She never wrote or visited.
Until now.

Wow.

I know.

And you weren't mad?

I was at first.
But mostly I just missed her.

I would've been mad.

Well, I can kind of understand.
Mom is a lot
sometimes.

I like your shirt today.

Thanks.
I like your headband.

Thanks.
It matches this bracelet
some girl gave me.

Some girl, huh?

Some girl.

• •

Kate

The squad is extra noisy today.

MDOMG!
The concert is so soon!
Well, not soon.
But soon-ish!
What are we going to wear?
Kate! What should we wear?

Hmm?

Um. To the concert.
On your birthday . . .
Hello, space cadet.

But that's so far away.

That's what I said!
It's not that far away.
She never pays attention anymore.
Earth to Kate!

Do we have to decide now?
What to wear, I mean?

UM, WHO ARE YOU?
WHAT HAVE YOU DONE TO KATE?
MDOMG.

The strange Kate is laughing.
She's a little familiar now.
Someone pull her ponytail.
See if she yells!

Fine. Fine. Fine.
Why don't you all come over?
We can figure out a plan.
Make T-shirts or something?
Yeah?

The squad disperses,
chattering down the hall
and I don't know what it is . . .
the mascot stuff?
Tam's pinkies?
Jill?
I'm feeling more and more . . .
apart from the squad somehow.

• •

Kate

I imagine Mom
at the dining room table
fingernails tapping
clacking
like they always do.

First I'll tell her about the squad,
the T-shirts,
she'll like that plan.

Then maybe we can talk strategy.
Mascot.
President.
Definitely not being captain,
but also definitely
not being regular.

And I can slip in the pinkies,
talk about Tam,
and how we're friends now,
and . . .

I imagine Mom's nails clicking faster,
her mouth in a line.
I imagine her head shaking,
matching the clacking,
and
ugh
It's all just . . .
too much.

Maybe . . .
maybe I'll leave it with the T-shirts.
For now.
No mascot stuff yet.

No president stuff yet.
Just one thing at a time.

But!
Maybe Tam can come make a shirt, too.
Then Mom will see we're *all* friends:
Me
and Tam
and the squad
and then one day it'll be easier
to talk to Mom like Jill said,
about the pinkies
and what that might mean
(if it means anything).
Yeah.
T-shirts now.
Mascot later.
Then pinkies.
Maybe.
One day.
Soon?

• •

TAM

Shortstack's been out of school
for at least a couple of days.
(Is it bad I don't know exactly
how long
it's been?)

(Is it bad that I only really noticed
today
that's he's been somewhere . . .
not here?)
I should go check on him,
make sure
he's breathin' easy.
And I will.
I'll go by after school.

Except.
I was going to see if Kate
wanted to hang out,
do some homework,
maybe
link a pinkie
or two.

• •

Kate

One little text.
That's all it takes.

Hey, Mom,
can the squad come over?
Make shirts?
For the concert?

Great!

she says.

And I wonder,
just for a second,
if maybe ALL our conversations
should be texting
because it's always somehow
so much easier.

• •

Kate

TAM

Sooooo, I know my mom scares you.

Almost as much as that gross
sandwich you're eating.

Shut up.
Hummus is delicious.
Anyway.
The squad is coming over
to make shirts.
And you
should come make one, too.

The squad?
Shirts?

For MisDirection.

MDOMG?!?!?!

Come on.
Don't make that face.

Why shirts?

So we'll stand out at the show.
So maybe the guys will see us.
And maybe they'll notice . . .

What?

Us!

And then what?

I . . .
I don't know . . .
I hadn't thought that far . . .

You're such a goof.

What!

Whaaaaat?

I don't sound like that.

Yes, you do.

Are you coming to make shirts or not?
It'll be good for Mom to see you again,
for you to jump back on the horse.

Do you really want me to?

Yes, Tam, of course.
I absolutely do.
I can even probably get you a ticket to the show
if you want me to.

Let's not go crazy.

Deal.

Deal.

• •

TAM

When someone sings
and their voice wobbles,
warbles,
goes off key . . .
that's what it's like right now,
me looking at me.
My reflection
in Frankie's pond,
my face,
warbling
up at me.
Who is that girl?
I thought I knew her,
but now I'm not so sure.
She's about to go make a T-shirt
for some boy band concert,
with a bunch of girls
she doesn't really know.
And she hates that band.
Like really a lot.
Their songs about love
and heart eyes
make no sense at all.
Plus Kate's mom will be there,
and when she sees the warbling face

of the girl in the pond
she's not going to like it,
not after last time.

I drop a rock in the pond,
watch as my wobbling face
turns to tiny waves,
ripples out,
disappears.

You're quiet today.

Frankie's shoulder knocks mine,
shoots a little energy into my arm.
My wobbling stops for a second.
I take a deep breath.
It's just a dumb shirt.
Just some girls hanging out.
No big deal.
Whatever.
This will be totally fine.

• •

Alex	Alyx	Alexx
An experiment.		
	So grand.	
		So bold.
Mixing Redwood and the squad.		
	So bold.	
		So grand.
Will it work? We do not know!		
	So bold.	
		So grand.
Let's watch and find out.		
	So grand.	
		So bold.

Kate

I stare at MisDirection
staring back at me.
Smooth faces.
Shining eyes.
Big smiles.
Except for Ben
the bad boy
who broods.
I stare at them and wait.
Should my heart beat faster?
Should my stomach twist?
Maybe if I stare longer
I'll understand.
Maybe if I keep faking it,
going all silly and giggly,
like Becca and the girls,
maybe I'll get it.
Maybe one day
my boy-crazy switch
will get flipped.
But right now
I stare,
waiting for something,
anything,
to happen,

and
well
nothing does.
My switch seems . . .
permanently off.

• •

TAM

She keeps looking at that poster
like maybe it will come alive,
maybe the boys will dive
into her room
zoom
her into their arms,
dance her
to the stars.
She stares at it and stares at it,
until I have to look away
because
dude
what's so great
about boys in a band?
What's so great
about their faces
looking so fake?

But she keeps looking at them
like they have the answers
to some great mystery,
like they
are the answers
to all the questions
in the universe.

• •

TAM

Puffy paints
T-shirt pens
giggling
giggling
giggling

Who is the cutest?
Joe
Pete
Ben
Max

giggling
giggling
giggling
and Kate giggles along with them
and I don't know why I think that's weird
because she IS one of them.
She's like, their leader, even.

And yet,
watching her
giggling
giggling
giggling
makes me wonder
who is this girl
sitting here
with paint on her cheek
laughing about *Joe's dimple*?
And why am *I* here
at all?

• •

TAM

Oh who am I kidding?
I'm here because she's here.
I'm here because
I get to hear
her laugh.
I get to see
her smile.
I get to smell
the ripple of air
when she walks by
that smells a little like
tangerines
and a lot like . . .
Kate.

I'm here to feel the warmth
when her elbow
accidentally brushes mine.
I just wish she'd look at me
instead of the poster
when she laughs
or smiles,
and maybe come near me
and possibly
actually
recognize that I'm
here
standing
in her room with
everyone else.

• •

Kate

Tam is so quiet,
fiddling with the bracelet I made her,
watching us all
like she's studying animals
in the zoo.
I wish she'd relax.
I wish she'd laugh.
I love it when she laughs.
It's like maybe a weird kind of music?

Is that a strange thing to say?
Out loud, I keep saying
funny things,
or things I think are funny,
but she doesn't laugh.
She doesn't even smile.
She's just watching us all
like we're aliens,
like her headband is on too tight
and all she wants to do is
rip it off
and throw it at us
and I can't quite figure out
why.

• •

TAM

Oh, Baby starts to play
and the girls all sing along
and Kate sings with them
loudest of them all
and for some reason
my ears start to burn,
my eyes start to sting,
my mouth opens up
and I act like I'm joking,
I smile like I'm teasing,

but my eyes,
my eyes
they just keep stinging,
as I keep talking.

For real, though,
let's talk about this poster,
this ridiculous boy band.
Let's talk about music
and how it shouldn't make girls
act dumb.
Let's talk about how fake these dudes are,
how they have goo-goo eyes.
Let's talk about why in the world you like them,
for real,
no lies.

• •

Kate

The squad looks at me
like Tam just peed in their cornflakes
and what can I do?
Confess that I, too,
don't care about this band?
That I would rather be
outside
under a tree
in the quiet
with Tam next to me?

Instead, I sigh.

Why are you so weird
about this dumb band?
(Becca sucks in her breath,
whispers, *so not dumb!*)
They sing catchy songs
and whatever.
You act like you'll die
if you hear one song.
Like your brain will melt
out of your ears,
why do you hate them so much?

• •

TAM

I keep talking
for way too long,
talking over
the confused questions
of the squad.

I don't get it.
She doesn't like MisDirection?
You don't like MisDirection?
But the songs are so fun.
It's not like they're Shakespeare.
And the boys are so cute!
If you don't like MD, then why are you here?

And it starts like I'm teasing,
but by the end it's not
and I don't understand
why I'm feeling so worked up
and I know I should
really
stop
talking
but I can't
because this is *Kate*.
And why is she acting so strange?
Why does her voice sound so high?
Why would she fall for a goofball band
and want to take the whole squad
to a show?
And I just don't get it,
I don't.
And now she's telling me to shut up
and she isn't smiling anymore
and I'm not sure what's happened
other than I've acted like a jerk
and she just walked me outside
and, uh,
I guess I'm going home.

• •

Kate

I don't want her to leave
but jeez
can't she just let it rest?
Why does it even matter what music I like?
Hasn't Tam ever exaggerated anything?
Hasn't she ever tried to fit in?
Probably not.
Because she's kind of perfect
just the way she is.
And now she's gone home
and I'm stuck here alone
with the squad
and they all think Tam is
bonkers.

How are you even friends with her
anyway?

She was just SO MEAN.
Does she talk like that ALL
the time?

And you sit with her at lunch—

—EVERY day?!

Why, Kate?

WHAT is going on?

I'm starting to realize
if I could really have my way
I'd be outside with Tam

and not stuck in here
with these girls and shirts
all day.
And Becca looks at me
like *I'm* the one
who peed
in her cornflakes
and I . . .
I start to feel this heaviness
in my chest,
the realization creeping in,
like I've lost something
and I have to sit down
because I have that
ripped-up feeling
again,
my insides like Mom's floor,
and can it be?
The heaviness inside is me
losing . . . *me.*

• •

TAM

I cross the street,
kicking my feet,
scuffing my shoes
on the rocks.

Whatever.
Whatever.

And the thoughts I hate
that I work so hard
to keep away
creep in
like the dust
my scuffing shoes
kick up.

Sure, I high-five everyone
in the halls at school
and Levi and I
are the masters of cool
but here's the real deal,
the actual truth:
I don't fit anywhere.
Especially with girls like that.
I've always been the one on the outside,
the weirdo book
that doesn't fit on any shelf.

• •

Kate

Mom eyes the paint on the newspapers
noting, I guess,
that my bedroom floor is safe
from paint
whew.
She asks if my new friend
—*Tam, Mom*—
had fun,
and says thank goodness
she's not as messy with paint
as she is with flour.
Mom asks if it bothers my new friend
—*Tam, Mom*—
to not be part of the squad.
She asks why my new friend
—*TAM, MOM*—
left early,
and makes sure I remember, right,
that there aren't any extra tickets,
for people who aren't on the squad?
She asks if I'm getting excited for my birthday,
excited for the show.
She's thinking of letting us all go
alone
because I'm such a leader
and she trusts me so much
and man . . .

my head throbs,
my stomach twists
as I realize
she'd never say that last part
to someone who's just a mascot.
Mascots aren't leaders.
Mascots are jokes.
Sigh.
It's not a good sign that
my plan to ease Mom
into all my new plans
has already
backfired.

• •

TAM

I feel so stupid.
The first words out of my mouth
when Frankie opens the door
and I storm in.
I really do.
Like,
am I jealous
of a poster?
Of a picture?
Of a bunch of dudes?
That doesn't even make any sense.

But like Mom says,
I am feeling my feelings right now,
and Frankie,
my feelings are that I could rip that poster
off that wall
wad it up
into a big stupid ball
and kick it
into the sun.

Those are strong feelings.

Duh, Frankie!
I know!

Hey. Watch your tone.

Sorry, I just . . .
I feel stupid.

What makes you feel stupid?

I don't know.
All of it.
Kate.
Everything.

I'm going to risk your wrath,
and ask
again:
What makes you feel stupid, Tam?

But I can't say
out loud
what I think I'm figuring out.
That I want Kate to look at me
like she looks at that poster.
That *I* want to be
her star.

I just do,
is what I actually say
and Frankie nods.
And I feel the feelings,
I feel the stupid,
I feel confusion and . . . shame?
I feel it crawling all over
my scrunched-up
face.

• •

TAM

Hey, Mom?
I just wanted to tell you
that I . . . I think I like Kate.
Like . . .
Like-like?
And—

What!?
First love!
Oh, Tam!
Oh, honey!
It's so exciting!
Have you told her?
Is she over the moon?
You know how lucky she is
to have you?

Good grief, Mom.
Stop.

Please.
I was going to say . . .
I think I like Kate AND . . .
I don't know what to do.
I went a little crazy.
Not in a good way.
I was mean to her for no reason
and, ugh.
What should I do?

Have you told her how you feel?
Talked it out? At all?
You can't know what she's thinking
or feeling
by just guessing,
you know.

What words would I even use?

Just tell her the truth.

But she was weird *today.*
Like someone I don't even know.
THAT Kate is not the one I like.
She really freaked me out.

Come here.
Give me a hug.
You're okay.
She's okay.
Don't make assumptions
about what people think.
You just have to talk to her . . .
okay?

• •

Alex

The electricity.

No zing.

Redwood leans.

Let's get closer.

Alyx

The air.

No crackle.

Ponytail wilts.

Let's watch out.

Alexx

Something different.

Something wrong.

Something weird.

Let's pay attention.

Kate

She's quiet today.
Even in the halls.
She's never quiet.
Especially in the halls.
She's not smiling.
Not even at Levi.
She never doesn't smile.
Especially at Levi.

At her locker
I bump her shoulder with mine.
She doesn't bump back.

Okay.
Something is definitely up.
Tam is definitely mad.

• •

TAM

It's not that I don't want to see her.
I always want to see her.
It's not that I don't like her.
I always like her.
It's not even that I'm mad.
Am I mad?

It's just . . .
which Kate am I going to see today?
MisDirection Kate?
Or my Kate?
And why are there so many
Kates?
And what am I supposed to say
about any of it?
I definitely don't want to say . . .
the *liking* thing.
Because seriously.
Who knows which Kate would hear me?
Who knows what she'd say?

• •

Kate

It's our Falcon Queen!

David yells
as I sit at the table
and pull out my sandwich.

But you better watch out
for that chicken head,

Mark laughs.

Did you see when he did that flip?
Whoever that kid is,
he's hilarious.

Then it's Mark and David
talk talk talking
about how great the fake
mascot is
while Becca interjects

Yearbook!

and blinds us all with her flash.
Super.
Awesome.
Just what I want.
Let's talk about the stupid fake mascot
and go blind from all the camera flashes
when I already don't want to sit here
to eat my stupid lunch.

Now even the squad joins in to laugh
until they see my face and stop,
except it's not the mascot
making me pout.

My three bites of sandwich
curl up in my stomach,
turn into rocks,
start to tumble
when I see Tam sit down,
so far away,
across from Levi,
a grin on her face.

Wow.
Look at her.
Laughing and chatting.
Levi makes her so happy,
and what do I do?
I make her mad.

• •

Kate

I can't figure it out.
What that kid has
to make Tam smile
so big
and laugh
so hard
every time
they're together.
I can't figure it out.
But I want to know.
What is the secret?
What is the magic
that gives Tam
the Levi glow?

• •

TAM

What's up, nerd?

Not much, turd.

Gonna give me a bite?

Only if you give me one first.

Levi snatches my pizza.
I grab his brownie.
It's been so long
since Levi and I were just . . .
me and Levi,
and I admit it's pretty nice
to sit and joke
and high-five
and be dorks.

But . . .

I see her.
Over his shoulder.
Ponytail swishing as she swats
David's arm,
smacks Mark's head,
giggles so loud
I could hear it a hundred miles away.

Hellooooooo.
It's like you're a hundred miles away.

Huh?

Earth to Tam.

Over and out, Levi.
Sorry, man.
I have to jet.

I jump up, grab my tray.
I can't sit here anymore
and listen to the noise.
I have to get out
before I go over there
and serve those boys
over the closest net
I can find.

• •

TAM

She catches my arm
as I rush into class,
hooks her pinkie in my bracelet,
holding me fast.

Hey.
What's up today?
Are you okay?
I missed you at lunch.

I'm fine.
It's nothing.
Plus, you sat with
the squad
first.

You're mad.

I'm not.

You are!
Why?
You know you can always come over,
you can always sit with us.

I pick at the puffy paint
still stuck to my thumb.

I don't know.
It's not that.
It's . . . the T-shirt making thing.
I guess I didn't have a very good time.

I could tell.
I'm sorry.
I thought it might be fun.
A girls' afternoon—

The thing is,
you're different around them.

What do you mean?
I'm always . . . me.

I shrug.

It just felt weird.
I felt weird.

Well that's no reason
to be mad at ME.

I said I wasn't *mad.*

I wanted you to be part of the group.
I wanted you to hang out with us.

I know.
It's fine.
It's just—the you I know
was different than the you
who showed up.

• •

Kate

What does she mean
the me she knows
is different than the me
who showed up?

My sandwich rocks threaten
to hurl themselves up my throat.

No one else seems to know
about the different Kates
and which one I choose to be,
but if Tam sees it
someone else will too
and then you know what will happen?

I will have to choose.
Which Kate is the real Kate?
What will I do?

• •

Kate

Other people are other people
who do other things
that you hear about
from other people
always talking about *they*.
And so what does it mean
when one day
the things other people say,
the things *they* do,
the things *they* are,
are the things *you* do,
the things *you* are?

What happens on the day
when *they*
become *you*
and the other people
other people talk about
are staring at you in the mirror,
that used to just show *your* face
instead of the face of *they*?

• •

TAM

You look embattled,
Grandneighbor.
What's going on?

Huh?

Troubled.
Worried.
Stressed.

Oh.
I don't know.
It's a lot of stuff.
I eat a Swiss roll.
Frankie watches me,
her hieroglyph eye
studying.

Frankie?

Hmm?

Does Roxy ever act weird?
When the two of you go out?

Roxy is always weird.

Ha.
I don't mean like that.
I mean . . . does she act like
someone else?
Or like she wishes you were
different?
More normal?

Frankie opens her mouth.
She doesn't say anything.
My stomach drops as I watch
her face
change.
I didn't mean normal,
I meant . . .

Roxy loves me as I am.
As I do her.

I nod.
Keep my mouth shut
before I say something
even more stupid.

• •

Kate

The driveway is three trucks deep
on my way home
from practice.
Floor guys.
Kitchen people.
A window thing.

It's so easy.
Too easy.
To text Mom,
to say:

I'm at the library
finishing up that project
pick me up later?

It's so easy
to text Jill
to say:
hey.
wanna get dinner?

And now here we are.
Cheeseburgers and milkshakes
again.

Can I ask you a question?
I blurt,
my mouth speaking
without permission.

Do you think it's bad
for there to be two of me?
Like . . . a cheer-me
and a Tam-me?
Because you didn't see
the meltdown that happened
with the MDOMG T-shirts,
and Jill,
I don't think I can figure out a way
for there to just be a me-me
who fits everywhere.

I don't know how to fit Tam
into all of my worlds,
so can't I keep her separate?
Do you think that would be okay with her?
Do you think that would work?

• •

Kate

I take it you haven't talked to
Mom.
About the pinkies?
About Tam?
About anything?

No.
There's just no way.
What would I even say?

I think you know
exactly
what you'd say.

But why does she need to know?

Don't you want her to know
who
exactly
you are?

No?

Oh, come on.
I know you do.

Don't let her bully you
into being someone
who isn't *you.*

• •

Kate

Bully ME, huh?
So when will you
tell Mom
your *secret, then?*
When will you tell her
you're back in town?

When will you talk to her
about Tam?

I know you don't get along,
but she'd probably like to know.

I know you're scared
to talk about your feelings,
but she'd probably like to know.

Are you ever going to tell her?

Are you?

If I do, will you?

Oooh. Interesting twist.
Okay, yes. Sure.
I will if you will.

Deal.
But who goes first?

• •

TAM

Hey, stranger.
Come here for a second?

I hold up my pinkie,
my Muppet voice says,

I brought you a cookie,
wanna go somewhere
and share it with me?

Kate looks around
like someone in a movie
being tracked by the CIA
then quickly holds up her pinkie
and quietly Muppet-voices:

Sure.

Kids move all around us,
running to the buses,
walking to their parents' cars,
so no one notices us
slip off to the grove of trees
behind the school.

We lean against a tree,
taking bites of the cookie,
sitting,
quiet,
shoulders touching.
She plays with the bracelet
on my wrist.

This thing is getting dirty,
you must really like it
to wear it so much.

I smile.
She grins back.
Time slows down
just a bit,
the clouds pause,
the sun sparkles,
I look at Kate, my Kate,
she looks at me back.
We hold our gaze for a long time,
until I lean in closer
and she leans in, too
and then I flick her nose hard
with the edge of my finger.

OW!

She pushes my shoulder,
and I fall to the side,
laughing so hard,

You had a bug on your nose!
I swear!

Kate grabs her nose,
giggling, too,
and shoves me some more
until we're both in the grass
looking up into the branches,
breathing fast.

• •

Kate

I know I'm acting weird,
I say to the clouds.
I'm sorry.
There's just a lot going on,
with this mascot stuff.
And I have to tell my mom
I don't care about cheer captain
anymore.
I think I'm going to run
for class president, instead.
Did I tell you that?
Honestly, Tam,
I don't know who to be.
I mean, of course I'm me.
It's just that the me I am
is usually the me Mom wants me to be.
It's all very confusing.
I've worked so hard to be the me

Mom wants
that I've never really thought of the me
I want.
What if my me isn't the cheer me or the captain me?
Or the possible president me?
What if my me is entirely different than the Mom-me?
And Tam . . . what if Mom doesn't like the me-me
just like she didn't like Jill's-me?
What if the me-me isn't as good
or smart
or perfect
as the Mom-me?
Then who will I be?
Nobody?

• •

TAM

Listen, if you figure out
the mom-you
isn't who
you are?
If you decide to
burn all that down
and start being who
you really are?
I'll be here to help you
put the fire out.

Burn it all down?

Just . . . when you're ready
to be you-you.
I'll be your girl,
right by your side.

My girl?

Yeah . . .
me-me and you-you.
Together-together.
That's what I mean.

Together-together.
I like how that sounds.
Pinkie-to-pinkie.

Pinkie-to-pinkie.

That's exactly what I mean.

• •

Kate

I love these moments,
the ones that feel like
everything
and everyone
disappears
and it's only us
in the whole world.
It makes me think that
if something feels
so perfectly right like this,
if the universe can hold us

in its hands like this,
then of course nothing's weird
or wrong
or different.
It makes me want to stay
right here
under this tree
forever
to memorize
how things
can be so simple
so normal
for just a minute
even when they aren't.

• •

TAM

President, huh?

Kate starts to laugh.
Her head leans into my shoulder.

I don't know what else to do.

Have you ever thought about doing less,
instead of more?

She just laughs harder.

Um, have you ever met my mom?

• •

Kate

Have *I* met my mom?
Am I really going to do this?
Am I really going to say it?
It's the only thing I can think about.
And Jill said she'll talk to Mom
if I do it first.
And Tam said she'd be by my side
if I want to be me-me.
And I think about sitting under the tree,
just Tam and me,
and how the world seemed
so simple and right . . .
and oh, man.
Here it goes.
I'm really going to do it.

Hey, Mom?
Mom?
What would you say
if I said
I think maybe
I'm, like,
I don't know
maybe
seventy-five percent
gay?

Mom?
Can you stop vacuuming?
Mom?
What would you say?

• •

Kate

You're not gay*, Katherine,*

is what she said,
whispering

gay

her face,
like stone,
her eyes,
like glass,
cool,
unblinking,
black.

Gay?

Still whispering.

You're too young to know . . .

that.

Still whispering.

Way too young
to be . . .

that . . .

Still whispering.

You're a normal girl.
A beautiful, smart leader.
Look at you!
Katherine.
Are you hearing me?
You're not gay.
What would people think?
There's just . . .
there's no way.
Okay?

Now it's my turn to whisper:
Okay.

Okay.

No more whispering.

Can you lift those couch cushions?
We need to straighten up around here.
I swear.
There's still flour everywhere.

• •

Kate

She says all these things
about laundry and dinner and
the grocery list and the mess
by the front door.
She doesn't look up as she moves
from room to room
picking up stuff
finding shoes

muttering about how I don't listen to her.
But she never looks at me.
She never sees me.
She doesn't understand
that if she took a breath,
stopped always moving and talking,
that she might see
the one who needs to be listened to
is actually me.

• •

Kate

I stare at myself
reflected in the toaster,
distorted.
Eyes huge,
chin small,
not like a human,
almost unrecognizable.
And for a second
my scalp tingles
when the thought skitters by
that maybe this is actually
how I look
to Mom,
to the world,
twisted up,
not right.

• •

Alex

Red alert.

A disturbance.

The forecast.

Red alert.

Alyx

Red alert.

A change.

Stormy.

Red alert.

Alexx

Red alert.

Divergence.

Watch out.

Red alert.

Kate

Her pinkie is relaxed.
She laughs,
talks to kids in the hall,
her finger gently holding mine,
keeping me close
so I can't escape.
But my pinkie holds onto hers
like it's holding onto a secret now,
holding its breath
afraid to move
afraid to get caught.
My heart starts to beat
faster
harder
scarier
and how did I never worry before?
About everyone seeing our pinkies?
About what they all might think?
Has everyone always seen the pinkies?
And no one said anything?
I mean, kids link pinkies sometimes,
so what.
Kids hold hands sometimes,
who cares?
Probably no one cares.
Probably I'm going crazy for no reason.
But then eyes catch mine.
Levi's eyes.

They dip down to the pinkies,
they look back up.
His mouth scrunches for a second
before he starts talking.

• •

TAM

I'm trying to get Levi
to finish his long story
by nodding
a lot
agreeing
on the spot
because I need him to be done.
Kate has eased away
and is already turning
so I can't see her face.
And where is she going?
I want to go with her.
Why did she let go of my hand?
Why won't Levi
stop
talking
just . . .

Hey!
Kate!
Wait!

I gotta go,
Levi.

I pretend his eyes don't narrow.
I pretend I don't see him shoot lasers
at Kate
as I run toward her.

Kate!
Wait!
Hey.

Hey.

Take a deep breath.
Are you okay?
Your face is like
white white white.
Here.
Sit down.
Have some water.
Kate.
Kate?

• •

Kate

Can everyone see me freaking?
I drink the water
sharing germs
sharing spit
sharing Tam

and it's like maybe a vitamin?
It makes me feel better,
stronger,
more like her.
I sip again.
More Tam.
Trying to be like her.
Trying not to care.
Trying not to see
everyone looking . . .
differently
at me.

I'm okay.
I say.

• •

Kate

She wants to know what happened
and I can't just say
I need a minute
to catch my breath.
I know it doesn't make sense
the cheerleader
the mascot
the possible future president
doesn't want eyes on her,
doesn't want people looking at her
staring at her

talking about her
whispering about her.
I know it doesn't make sense
and I need to figure it out
and I don't know what to say
so I blurt:

Maybe people are looking too much.
At us.
Maybe linking pinkies is weird.
Maybe we should stop.

Her face gets kind of frowny.
She says,

Since when are you afraid of
people looking at you?
At us?

Her forehead wrinkles,
her eyebrows dip low,
confusion passes over her face
like a shadow.

What's going on?

I don't know what to say.
Mom says I can't be gay?

Tam's arms cross over her chest,
a wall I've not seen before
and I feel a jab
in my stomach
like a punch,
a blow.

I don't know,
I just . . .

Hey. Listen.
Deep breaths.
It's okay.
No more pinkies.
If that's what you want.

And I know,
even though she's being nice,
those few little words
I blurted just now . . .
I've just . . .
Man.
I really let her down.

But GAH.
That freaks me out, too,
because I *want* to hold hands
except now,
sigh.
I'm afraid to.

• •

TAM

I want her to be happy
and smiley
and goofy.
I want her to be the Kate

I know.
I want all of those things.
So if I need to stop holding her hand
to make her happy
then fine.
I'll do that.
But I admit
I don't understand.

Not holding hands
doesn't feel happy
or
smiley
or goofy.
It just feels sad.

• •

Kate

I don't want her strong
slim pinkie
to intertwine with mine.

I don't want her palm
just a little bit sweaty,
pressed against mine.

I don't want to feel
the heartbeat in her thumb
beat beat beating along with mine.

I don't want to hold her
smooth, soft hand
tightly against mine.

If I wanted all of that,
what kind of girl would I be?
Definitely not the normal kind.

• •

TAM

It's okay she disappeared
right in front of me.
People are weird,
right?

It's okay she barely ate,
barely talked,
and then left me.
Right?

It's okay she didn't say goodbye,
she didn't look at me,
or smile one time.
Right?

Whatever.
I'm sure
it's fine.

Right?

• •

Kate

Becca pulls me aside,
fingers pressing
into my upper arm
squeezing,
yanking,
dragging me
away.

Her eyes are wide,
as she shoves me
into the bathroom.

Hey.

Um. Hey?
I rub my arm
where her fingers just squeezed.
Is there an emergency?

I just heard something.

Okay?
Her eyes are wide.
Concerned.

Jeremy said
Paul said
Kaitlyn said
Chloe saw you
and Tam
kissing
after school
the other day.

My whole body goes tingly
like static shocking
every inch of my skin
as I literally feel the blood
in my face
drain
away.

What?
My voice chokes out,
like the words are made of
sand.
That's crazy.

That's what I said.
Why would you kiss someone who
yelled at all your friends?
Why would you kiss someone who
was
so MEAN?

Becca looks at me like
I'm a book written in French
she's trying really hard
to understand.

So it's not true?

Of course it isn't!

It isn't.
But my face flames when I realize
I wish it was.

Okay. Well, weird.
Why would she say that?

I don't know.
But it's one hundred percent
untrue.

Cool.

Cool.

But nothing,
nothing,
feels cool,
especially my cheeks
and the boiling burning
churning
of my stomach.

• •

Kate

Jill's car pulls up
outside of school,
her smile big,
her silver glitter eye shadow
raining down her cheeks
when she blinks.

Need a ride?

She knows I need a ride.
We already planned this.
My arms are crossed so tight
they hurt my chest.

Kate?
Hop in.
Milkshakes on me.

I chew the inside of my lip.
Stare at her face.
It's longer now,
where it used to be
round
it's . . . different.
She looks like a grown-up
and I guess she is.
Sort of.

I told Mom.

The words come out on their own.

I told Mom.
She didn't care.
I mean worse than that . . .
she just said . . .
no.
She told me I'm wrong.
About my own self!
And she asked what people would think.
And I hadn't thought about that,
not a whole lot,
Jill,
what would *people think?*
Then today,
I asked Tam to stop,
no more holding hands
until I can . . .
I don't know,
figure out my thoughts
and
THEN I found out
there's this rumor—
I feel like I might choke
and throw up
or worse
cry.

Oh.
Oh, hey.
Kate.

The engine stops
just like my heart,
and she jumps from the car,
opens my door.
Her arms swoop around me,
warm and tight
and she doesn't say anything
just holds me
in front of everyone
like someone has died.

• •

Kate

Why did I listen to you, again?
Why did I think that was a good idea?
You, who left us.
You, who Mom hates.
Why did I do the thing
YOU said to do?
I *can't leave, Jill!*
You know that, don't you?
I can't just pack a bag and run off.
I'm not eighteen like you were.
I have nowhere to go.
I don't even want *to go somewhere else.*
I just want Mom to listen.
I just want to be heard.

Why aren't I as important as
the brand-new
stinking
floors?

• •

Kate

The milkshake is melted.
Slimy
warm
pukey pink.
I imagine that my guts look like this, too.
The inside of my heart
just mixed-up slop.

I look up.

Jill hasn't said anything.
She just keeps looking at me.
Nothing is right.

And then
without even thinking
my hand swats out,
smashes into the milkshake
spraying it
all over Jill's shirt

all over her stupid glittery face
and I stand up
and I walk out.

• •

Kate

She's behind me
her boots clip-clop
like a military horse.

I swipe at the tears
and I wish,
oh I wish,
they would turn to tiny daggers
so I could spin and throw,
hit her with my sorrow.

Kate. Please. Stop.

Kate. Please. Stop.
It feels like those are the only words
anyone ever says to me.
Kate, don't do that.
Kate, do this other thing.
Kate, you're better than that.
Kate, look at what you can be.

Look at what I can be.
Something no one likes
or believes.
This girl,
this stupid girl,
with deviant pinkies.

• •

Kate

I'm only here because I'm not going home.
I'm only here because I started to get cold.
I'm only here because Jill followed me.
I'm only here because she made me get in the car.
I'm only here because I don't know where else to go.
I'm not here because I want to talk.
I'm not here because of the cocoa.
I'm not here because she keeps hugging me.
I'm not here because she's quiet.
I'm not here because I've missed her more than I can know.
I'm not here because I've forgiven her
for her terrible, hideous advice.
I'm only here because I had to go to the bathroom
and at least her bathroom is nice.

• •

Kate

Tell me what you want
Jill said
right now.
Today.
What do you want
to make you happy?
And I said
for everyone I love to be happy.
And she said
but what would make you happy?
And I whispered
what if me being happy
makes everyone else unhappy?
And she said
it never would
And I whispered
we can't all be happy at the same time
And she whispered
your happiness makes other people happy, Kate
And I whispered
I don't think so
in a voice that was barely anything at all.
And she hugged me.
And I cried.

• •

Kate

Everything is quiet
on our drive home.
Me sniffling a little,
Jill glancing at me,
the corner of her eye
getting quite
the workout.

When the car slows down
a block from the house
so Mom can't see
me
getting out,
I finally turn to Jill,
feeling so tired,
so sad.

I did my part.
Our stupid plan, remember?
Now it's your turn, Jill.
Don't make me tell her
something else she doesn't want
to hear.

• •

Kate

Mom's face
when Jill comes through the door,
it breaks.
It collapses in on itself,
crumbling.
A wall
torn down.

Mom's face
when her hands clap over her mouth
and her eyes swim
swim
swim
until they spill over her hands,

Mom's face
buried
in Jill's shoulder
as Jill looks over at me
and our eyes lock,
holding each other just as tight
as Jill holds Mom.

• •

Alex	Alyx	Alexx
It's not better today.		
	It's worse.	
		So much worse.
The world off-kilter.		
	A freak-out.	
		Threatening.
I can't bear it.		
	My stomach hurts.	
		Look away.

Kate

When you take a deep breath,
really do it right . . .
Inhale
1
2
3
4
5
Exhale
1
2
3
4
5
That deep calm you feel,
that steady moment,
calm,
clear,
is how I feel
when I know Tam is near.

But then I notice
everyone noticing
me noticing Tam
and I can tell
they can tell
something is different,
that she's not a regular friend.

And then I feel kind of scared.
And I don't know why.
And I push Tam away.
And the calm and clear
disappears.
I *want* to talk to her,
to tell her about things at home.
And I want Tam to know
I think about her
all the time.
And I want to explain that
I don't know what to do about it
and that I'm afraid
of being different
even more than I'm afraid
of Mom.

• •

TAM

I'm cool.
It's a regular day.
Nothing weird happening
at
all.
I'm high-fiving.
I'm strutting.
And look,
it's Kate and the squad.

Might as well say hey,
see what they're doing,
try not to mention MisDirection
or act supremely stupid.
I'll dig my pinkies
in my pockets
so no one can see them.
Just a regular morning.
Yep.
Gonna go hang with the squad.

• •

Kate

Tam is acting super strange,
talking really loud,
laughing even louder.
She just actually said,

What's the haps?

to Becca
and Becca looked at me
like
Get this crazy girl out of here.
I throw a marker,
hit Tam in the back of the head,
she yells,
turns around,
her smile is . . .

too big,
almost scary
or
scared?

Hey,

she says.

What are you doing?
Can I help?

The squad looks panicked,
but I still say yes.
We can all make posters together.
Just . . . regular friends.

• •

TAM

Everything
continues
to be great,
I keep saying
in my head.
Look at me
and the squad,
a big bunch
of friends.

We make posters
for the election,
each one
with Kate's face.

There's no way
she can't win.
Three cheers
for Team Kate.

• •

TAM

I sneak looks at her
across the table,
hoping to catch her
sneaking looks at me, too.
Just one smile
between us
that's all I need.
Just one smile.
Not even fancy.
Just a little sideways grin.
Like she knows a secret
and I know it, too.
She never looks, though.
Not at me.
Not once.
I pluck at the bracelet on my wrist,
snap
snap
snap
and just for a second
I want to throw it

right at her
just to get her attention.

• •

Kate

I know she's looking at me,
but I can't look back.
If I look,
my pinkie will be lonely.
I'll want to throw the posters away.
I'll want to forget about everything,
I won't care what people say.
But I do care.
I want them to think of me as
Mascot Kate
or
President Kate
or
Cheer Kate
or even regular Kate.
Not
Gay Kate.
No way.
Gay Kate
is too different
and different messes up
everything.

• •

TAM

I
snap
snap
snap
my bracelet
as I walk
to Frankie's.

I
just
just
just
can't see
what's different now
than under the tree.

I
don't
don't
don't
understand
what's happened.

I
thought
thought
thought
we decided to be . . .

I don't know.
I guess I'm missing
something.

• •

Kate

Where's your new BFF?
We could use her right now.
Yeah! She's so tall.
Figures she'd just leave.
Kate. Hand me the tape.
Kate!
Kate, are you listening at all?

My Redwood is gone,
out the door,
long
legs
carried her away.
I wish I'd said bye
or even hello
or something
anything.
But I didn't.
I couldn't.

It's just . . .
ugh . . .
it's easier to be

non-pinkie friends
if I don't actually *see* Tam
as much.

Tape?
It's right here.
And hey, can you fix that poster?
It needs to be perfect, and
it's not straight at all.

• •

TAM

Meercat stands on three legs,
one claw raised
to the bright light in his cage,
lizard yoga.

I stare at the light,
so bright,
and when I look away
a black spot
throbs
in both eyes
erasing the middle
of everything.

This is how I spend my days,
I say to Frankie,
watching the blob
blacken the room.
I'm missing something big,
right in front of me
but out of reach.
Something that I guess
only Kate can see.

• •

Kate

I've never noticed how wide
Coach's eyes can get
until today when I told her
I don't want to be captain.
She seemed to lose her words,
just nodded as I talked,
as I told her I'm ready to go big,
be president,
and have fun
as mascot.

That's really bold

is what she said.

And your mom is on board
with all of this?

Of course,
I lied.
She's really excited.
She wants me to be happy
and when I said happy
my voice kind of choked
making me cough,
tears rising
until I swallowed
hard,
composed myself.

You're sure about this?

Coach's wide eyes
went soft.

Everything's okay?
Nothing's wrong?

I nodded,
throat tight,
burning from before.

We'll still have to have tryouts.
For mascot.
I can't just give you the
permanent job.
But you'll do fine, I know.

I nodded again.
Tryouts.
I forgot about that part.

Now I'm in my room,
figuring out how to tell Mom

I was just kidding
probably
about that gay thing,
and that
I just killed her dream of captain,
but for presidential
reasons.

• •

TAM

Mom.
Please.
Mom.
Listen.

. . . and Kate and her mom
can come over
for dinner!
Won't that be —

Mom.
Stop.
I don't think . . .

What's the problem?
It'll be so fun!
Girlfriends and Momfriends!

MOM!
NO!
UGH!

Hey there, you.
Watch that tone.

Sorry.
It's just . . .
let's not make any dinner plans
with them
just yet.
I'm . . .
I'm going to my room.

Oh. Okay, baby.
Is everything—

It's fine.
I'm fine.

• •

Kate

We aren't holding hands
anymore.

Sorry?

Jill is making popcorn
for movie night
just me and her
and Mom.
Should be great.
Sigh.

Me and Tam.
That's done.

No more pinkies.
I thought you'd like to know.

What happened?

I give her a look.
She knows exactly what happened.
She gives me a look back.

You need to be yourself.
Don't hide behind something
you're not.

Mom walks in
saying something about
popcorn on the floor.

Kate.
Did you hear me?

I did.
But I pretend I don't.

• •

Kate	TAM
Maybe I'll stay right here in my room	Maybe I'll stay in my room right here

for a while.

Maybe if I close my eyes curl up tight I'll figure out what to do.	Maybe if I curl up tight close my eyes I'll figure out what Kate wants.

• •

Alex

Did you see?

The posters.

Have we noticed?

So many.

Do you wonder?

What they say?

Let's read between the lines.

Alyx

Did I see?

The posters.

Did you see?

So many.

Do I wonder?

What they mean?

Let's read between the lines.

Alexx

Have we noticed?

The posters.

Did I see?

So many.

Do we wonder?

Why so many?

Let's read between the lines.

TAM

Kate!
Hey!
Kate?
Hello?

I guess she didn't hear me.
Or see me.
In class.
Or at lunch.

I guess she's pretty busy
running
for president.

I guess if I'm telling the truth
she seems even busier
running
from me.

• •

Kate

If I stay away,
don't engage,
leave Tam to do her own thing,
then people will stop talking about us,
and everything will be okay.

I'll get more posters up on the walls,
kill it with this presidential campaign.
I'll be back to the Kate
everyone knows.
That has to be the right choice
to make.

• •

Kate

I mean, what is a friend,
anyway?
Can't anyone be a friend?
In the grand scheme of things?
Can't you eat lunch with whomever you want?
Hang out with,
chat with . . . anyone?

Even if the air in the room seems stale
or your stomach clenches shut
or your soda loses its taste.
I mean, it's just lunch.
Eat with anyone.
Be with anyone.
What does it matter?
It's no big deal
sitting with the squad
sitting with Becca and the girls.
It shouldn't make me
even sadder.
They're my friends.
Just like they always were.

• •

TAM

Cool.
No Kate again today.
Lunch has become
my least favorite part
of the day.

• •

TAM

Everywhere I look,
posters with Kate's face.
It's like some kind of mean joke:
the more she dodges me in the halls
the more I see her IN THE HALLS.
Her pretty face,
her blank eyes,
staring,
following,
watching me.

That day under the tree
I thought she said
we would be . . .
something
something more
something more than friends.
Her-her.
Me-me.
Together-together.
But I guess that was then.
And now?
I only ever see her
in two dimensions.
Ugh.
Please tell me that's not
how it's always been.

Please tell me I haven't imagined
the fun and laughs
and easy times.
Please tell me it wasn't pretend.
If it was all fake,
I don't know what I'd do.

• •

Kate

No more cafeteria for me.
I need
lunchtime
to practice my mascot
routine.
I need
lunchtime
to practice my election day
speech.
I need
lunchtime
to practice being
the right kind of
me.

• •

TAM

Sometimes,
out of the blue,
around a corner,
when I catch her off guard,
I see my Kate
in her eyes
and she smiles.

But then she stops fast
as if a slap,
a cold splash
has woken her up,
and as quickly as it appeared,
her smile is gone.

• •

Kate

It shouldn't be true.
I'm busy all day every day.
I'm friends with nearly everyone
in school.
My ponytail bobs
with just the right swish.

My election posters are a perfect mix
of cute
and funny
and serious.
And yet somehow,
the real truth is
all I am is sad.
I'm just so sad now
all the time.
Even with the game tonight
and another chance
to kill it as mascot,
I can't shake this feeling of
ugh.
I can't find the right smile.
I try to be like the squad.
I try to be what Mom wants.
But I think something inside me is broken
because nothing fits anywhere anymore.
My ponytail is the same.
My bow just as tight.
But if you could see through my eyes
you'd see nothing is right.

• •

Kate

I look through the Falcon's eyes
hoping that might fix things,
let me be me
in disguise.
But that stupid chicken head runs by
and the crowd goes nuts.

I could chase him,
but no.
I don't want to be part of
his stupid show.
Honestly, I just want to
get out of here.
I'm over it.
I want to go home.

• •

TAM

I didn't tell her I'd be here
to watch her
instead of the game,
but here I am
and that chicken head

is once again
on the field.

And I want to tell Kate
she shouldn't care.
She should keep working hard,
keep doing the thing she loves,
forget about the chicken,
she's such a good mascot.

But by the time the game is over
and I get down to the squad,
she's already gone
flown the coop,
swept away by her mom.

• •

TAM

You've been busy, huh?

The next day
I don't know
what else to say.
I don't know
how else to say it.

I swallow
all my questions,
they break up
inside me
shards
poking
scratching
stabbing,
my guts hurting.
I want to ask:
Are you mad?
I want to ask:
Why?
Where have you been?
I miss you.
Do you miss me, too?
But I don't say anything else.
I swallow the words whole.
I feel them shatter
in my throat
as she looks past me
eyes blank
and says,

Not too busy.
What's for lunch today?

• •

Kate

I'm right here
and she isn't listening.
She doesn't hear me.

TAM

I'm right here
she doesn't see
and she won't look at me.

What exactly
is happening?

Kate:

I want her to hear
to understand.
I need room to breathe.
I need some space
to see
what's what

TAM:

I want her to see
to understand.
I need her close to me.
I need her smiling face
to be
right here

right now.

Kate:

I'll find her
when I'm ready

TAM:

We can talk.
I'm ready.

I promise.

• •

TAM

She wears her cheerleader camouflage
and it works like magic.
They all think they know her
just like I thought I did.
Except . . .

I guess the Kate I know
isn't the Kate I thought she was.
It looks like the squad knew
the real Kate
and *I* was fooled
by her other camo.

I just don't understand you,

is all I can say
to Kate
as I walk by
and she flips her ponytail
and Becca stares straight
ahead.

• •

Kate

Tam doesn't understand.
Tam doesn't understand?
TAM DOESN'T UNDERSTAND!?
GAH
I COULD SCREEEEEAAAAM!
Of *course* she doesn't!
She never could!
Things are so easy for her!
She just does her thing!
Tam is Tam!
No one cares!

She knows what she wants!
So she gets what she wants!
How?! Beats me!
Everything
EVERYTHING
is so easy
for Tam!
So of *course* she doesn't understand!
She can't, can she?
Tam has never,
not once,
even tried to think about
what it must be like
to be
me!

• •

TAM

What is she doing over there?
All those markers?
All that poster board?
Please tell me . . .
No.

I grab Levi,
toss him on my shoulders,
run by,
take a look.

More posters?!
They're already EVERYWHERE.
We get it, Kate.
Jeez.

Seeing more
of her empty face
in the halls?
That's one hundred percent
the last thing
I need.

• •

Kate

Like she's fooling anyone
running past the table
pretending she isn't paying attention.

Well I'm not paying attention to her either.
I don't notice her either.
My heart doesn't leap—
my palms don't sweat—
my head doesn't get tingly—
either.

Nope.
Not at all.
None of those things.
Don't even see her.

• •

TAM

When the idea hits,
I laugh out loud
and almost get a detention
because everyone turns around
to look at me,
but I don't care.
Because I am about to serve up
the biggest spike of my career.

I admit I don't really care
about being school president
at all,
but if I have to see Kate's face
every day
plastered all over the walls,
then guess what,
I'm running, too,
a late entry to the game.

I'll have posters, too.
She'll have to see me everywhere, too.
All is fair,
you know,
in love
and
war
and
presidential campaigns.

• •

Kate

WHAT.
She's running against me?!
HOW?
WHY?
There's no way she'll win.
What a joke.
Everyone knows
she's not serious about it,
everyone knows
I'm in it to win it.
Everyone knows she's just doing this
to get to me
except
wait
why would everyone know
that?

• •

Alex | **Alyx** | **Alexx**

Alex: Is this the end?

Alyx: Their story is over?

Alexx: No more Redwood and Ponytail?

Alex: It had such promise.

Alyx: It was really going places.

Alexx: How can we survive?

Alex: Our poor duo.

Alyx: Our lovely stars.

Alexx: Their shine is lost.

TAM

Meercat sits on my jeans,
nibbling at my bracelet,
looking up at me
eyes black
unblinking
seeing
everything
inside.
And Frankie,
her eyes are the same,
staring
seeing me
inside out
while I sip tea
and discover
for once
I don't have the words
to explain
what I'm feeling.
I don't know how to say
anything.

• •

TAM

It's like she pulled me closer
so we could be friends,
then she pushed me away

and pulled me closer again.
What am I?
Some kind of yo-yo friend?

Frankie nods.
She makes more tea.
She's quiet,
letting me do the talking.

Until . . .

I'm going to tell you a story, Tam.
It may apply to you.
It may not.
But I'm going to tell it, okay?
My story.
Do with it
what you may.

It took me a long time to admit
to myself
my true identity.
Which makes me sound
like a superhero.
Spoiler: I'm not.

This made me very sad
for a very long time,
trying to hide.
I didn't want to be me.
I worked very hard
to be someone else.

I worked so hard at that,
I married a boy I'd known
my whole life.
We had three boys of our own.
Our life was the way lives are:
A house
two cars
soccer after school
dinner in the crockpot.
But I always knew
deep in my heart
something didn't fit.

I
didn't
fit.

It's very hard to explain
to your family
that you don't fit
when you've spent decades
working very hard
to pretend that you do.

Imagine carefully twisting
a balloon
into just the right shape,
like at a birthday party,
but the shape isn't perfect,
so you twist it again,

you try a new shape,
but it still doesn't quite work,
so again
and again
you twist
and contort
until the balloon . . .
it just can't twist anymore,
and it pops
right in your face.
Bam.

Folks get scared.
They get mad.
They get sad.

Overnight everything changes.
Even with dinner still
in the crockpot.
Even with soccer after school.
But even with so many scattered
pieces of balloon,
you learn, over time,
those scattered pieces . . .
they're all still you.

Now. Would I have changed anything?
Would I have made different choices
as a young girl who didn't know
what to do?

I don't know.
I only wish I'd had an old lady
friend
with a lizard and a pot of tea . . .
someone who would listen.
And maybe Kate doesn't have that.
Maybe she's still twisting her balloon,
maybe she's still learning about
which shapes she might choose.

• •

TAM

I've known Frankie
my whole
entire
life
and those
are the
most words
I've ever heard
come out of
her mouth
at once.

• •

TAM

Thank you.

It's the only thing
I can think to say.

Thank you for the tea.
Thank you for the words.
Thank you for the lizard break.
I . . .
I . . .
It's time for me to go home.
For some reason, I just . . .
I really want my mom.

• •

TAM

Baby, what's wrong?

Mom's hands
on either side of my face;
her eyes
try to pull answers
from me.

Baby.
Tell me.

But what can I say?
That Kate's afraid to like me
the way I like her,
or maybe she never has
liked me . . . in that way
at all?
That I'm running against her
for president
just so she'll see me
because I didn't know what else to do
and now I just feel . . .
stupid.
It's too much to say,
too much to believe.
The words pile up in my throat,
too many to escape
so I say
nothing,
I just let Mom hug me.
I just feel the feelings
even though right now
I pretty much
don't want to feel
anything
ever
again.

• •

Alex **Alyx** **Alexx**

Alex: What happens now?

Alyx: It's anyone's guess.

Alexx: We'll keep watching.

Alex: This schism.

Alyx: This break.

Alexx: This mess.

Alex: Redwood's broken.

Alyx: Ponytail's split.

Alexx: Two are ones again.

Alex: A bummer.

Alyx: A heartbreaker.

Alexx: A tragedy in the making.

Kate

Every day
so boring
so same.
I put up more posters,
go to class,
practice,
then home
and bed
and toss and turn
and start again.

I can laugh and hang out,
make posters,
pretend like it's okay
but deep down inside
I miss Tam more
every day.

I'm trying to be the Kate
everyone wants me to be.
I'm trying to be the best
everything
I can possibly be.
But it's like my eyes were opened
for just a little while
and now I can't unsee the world
that Tam's Kate saw.

I miss it.
I miss Tam.
I miss that me.
I miss it all.

• •

TAM

I don't love space.
I don't even need it.
But I have it.
Big wide open fields
of space
all around me.

Just me
myself
and
I.

Even Levi wants space
from me,
Tam the Jerk.
After I ignored him for so long.
I guess he's had enough.

So I make posters of my face,
put them up all over,
VOTE FOR TAM!
SHE'S YOUR (wo)MAN!

and I just . . .
float around,
drowning
in all of this space.

• •

Kate

What will I do when I'm president?
Hmm.
Writing this speech is supposed to be easy.
I have the votes I need already.
At least I think I do.
Tam has no experience.
And the other kid running . . .
whatshisname,
no one even knows who he is.
All I have to do
is give a speech
just before the vote.
It should be simple,
easy,
so why am I staring at this paper
like
I've never written words
before?

• •

TAM

A speech, huh?
In front of the whole school?
How hard could it be?
All I have to do
is ask them to vote for me.
Maybe I would care more
or be nervous
or whatever
except
the only part
giving me a spinning heart
is the idea
that Kate will be sitting by me
on stage,
in the next chair.
My pinkie might want to say hi
and hers definitely won't
and ugh
who thought running for president
was a good idea
because now I sure don't.

• •

TAM

Out of nowhere
I hear her name over the P.A.
asking her to go see the vice principal
right now.
What could *that* be about?
Maybe they want her to know
she has too many posters,
a violation
of some kind of
that's-enough-of-your-face rule.
But what if it's an emergency?
What if something happened to her dad
or Jill?
Or there was a freak house remodel accident
and her mom has been impaled
by flooring
and is pinned to a wall?
Kate gets up from her desk,
rushes to the office,
and I wish
I wish
I could rush with her.
I want to make sure she's okay.
It would kill me if she was hurt.

• •

Kate

They're calling me down to the office . . .
Am I in trouble?
What is it?
What could I possibly have done?
Did someone somehow find out
that I might want to kiss a girl?
Do they know I feel sick every day?
That all I think about is Tam?
That even when I try not to think about her,
I'm still technically thinking about her
and it's the worst torture
ever?
Maybe the school doesn't want me
to be president
because of my deviant pinkies.
Maybe they called Mom.
Maybe they think I'm totally broken
and this is only a school for
regular whole kids?

But when I get there,
totally out of breath,
my brain whirling and burning,
thinking that I've been caught,
am in trouble,
that everyone has figured me out,
I see . . .

Levi.
A sad frown on his face,
he can barely look at me.

And my entire insides turn to ice,
I have to grab the wall,
because if Levi is here
and Tam isn't
then that means
something has happened to her,
something . . .

• •

Kate

The vice principal starts talking,
interrupting my racing thoughts,
and

oh

come

ON.

Shut

the

front

DOOR.

THIS IS WHY I'M HERE?
Are you *KIDDING* me?
THAT little flea?
HE'S the one?
The creep stealing my show?

All thoughts of Tam
and pinkies
and secrets
and president
fly out of my brain
and everything is replaced
with burning
angry
flames.

Levi is the chicken head?
He's been the fake mascot this whole time?
THAT'S why I'm here?
So he can apologize?
Oh good grief,
I just . . .
I can NOT.

• •

TAM

His voice is squeaky
over the intercom
when they make him apologize to Kate

and blast it
to the whole school.

Oh, man, oh, man,
shortstack, no.
Levi, why?
Oh man, oh no.

As soon as the bell rings
I run down the hall,
see Kate
and before I can say
anything
she hauls back
and
SMACK
a slap
heard round the world.

Yearbook!

Becca yells,
flash flash flash.

Levi is stunned,
a pink handprint bright
on his face,
as Kate whips around,
marches off,
with a fierce ponytail swish.

• •

Alex	Alyx	Alexx
It was just a boring day.		
	One of many boring days.	
		They're mostly boring days.
They're mostly boring days.		
	It was just a boring day.	
		One of many boring days.
Until.		
	Until.	
		Until.
That announcement.		
	The slap heard round the world.	
		The talk of the school.
The talk of the school.		
	That announcement.	
		The slap heard round the world.

Hold onto your seat.

Grab a snack.

Things are heating up.

Things are heating up.

Hold onto your seat.

Grab a snack.

Redwood.

Ponytail.

They're on the attack.

Kate

I got to hide
under the Falcon head,
under its wings.
I got to be silly,
jump around,
be me-me.
And stupid Levi,
stupid, stupid Levi,
he *stole* that from me.
He is *always* himself,
always Tam's friend,
always the king of the halls,
he knows *exactly* who he is.
So why would he need a mask;
why would he steal my show?
There's no reason at all.
Except . . .
I mean . . .
unless he was in my brain,
he had no idea
his stupid chicken head
was stealing me from me.
And now Tam.
She's doing the same thing!
Stealing my presidency,
while barely even trying.
Well, we'll see about that.
My posters are on fire.

She can't beat me at this,
no way
no how
it's not even an option.

• •

TAM

I feel like
I should say something
about Levi's mascot thing,
even though
I didn't know.
I have this itchiness
like it's somehow
partly my fault.
I walk up behind her,
ready to tap her shoulder,
try to talk,
when I hear:

She doesn't know anything
at all
about being president.
I mean,
come on.
She probably thinks
class president
can do dumb things
like tell teachers what to teach
and get soda in the cafeteria.

Everyone around her laughs
as she flips her ponytail
and my mouth goes dry.

She has no idea
what she's doing.
I'm not worried.
Seriously.

Seriously?
I back away
before she can see me.
Fine.
That's how we're doing this?
Cool.
I crumple my election speech,
crushing it in my pocket.
Yeah. We'll see who
doesn't know
what she's up against.

• •

Kate

Tam sits next to me
onstage
and doesn't say a word,
she just stares ahead,
hands in her lap.
I wonder if she's nervous
or if it's the same as a game.

I wonder if she'll be cool and confident
just like when she wins a point,
makes the crowd go nuts.

That whatshisname kid,
the third candidate,
just finished his speech and
yawn
I'm gonna dust him
like a powdered donut.

I shuffle the note cards in my lap,
smile to myself
because, yeah
my speech is so good,
it's totally on point.
I have this election won already.
But first I have to be poised,
look happy,
listen politely
as Tam takes the podium.

She winks at me
as she stands up
and of course
of course
my traitorous stomach
flip-flops twice
even as I try to ignore

the jolt
that always hits
when Tam's eyes
lock onto mine.

Why would she wink?
Is she trying to throw me off?
Well, it won't work.
I close my eyes.
I'm cool.
I'm collected.
I'm winning this thing,
no questions asked.

• •

TAM

I look out over the whole gym
full of the entire school.
Then I look directly into
Kate's eyes
as I say,

I will make sure we get sodas
for free
in the cafeteria
every day.

Everyone cheers,
a thundering crowd
and I pause as I keep my eyes
on Kate.

I say,
I will also make sure we have
no more tests
ever
on Fridays.

I hold up my hand
to stop the cheers
as I continue,

I promise free tickets to concerts
for getting straight As,
and if you get Bs
you can still come,
you just have to stand
farther from the stage.

The entire gym bursts into applause
as they chant my name.

Oh!

I shout,
quieting them down,

One more thing:
Every kid gets their own cheerleader,
who has to do what they say.

The crowd laughs and claps,
cheers and whistles,
while I fling my arms in the air,
V for Victory
and walk right past Kate.

She smooths her skirt as she stands,
and whispers fiercely to me:

You can't do any of that.
None of those promises are real.

I shrug.

Yeah, I guess I don't know
anything about anything.
Except . . .
I do know
what a crowd wants to hear.

• •

Kate

That Tam,
that girl,
that
that
that

ARGH!
She isn't playing by the rules,
she's making ME look bad.
My speech is about
community service,
about making the school a better place,
and no one cares at all
because I haven't mentioned sodas once
and I can't control when tests will be given
BUT NEITHER CAN SHE.
Oh good grief,
my speech is done.
Hello?
No one even heard me.

• •

TAM

Maybe it was mean
to make promises I can't keep,
but the look on her face . . .
it was sort of worth it
when I waltzed past.
Her eyes shooting fire,
her cheeks burning pink,
her mouth scrunched up
and all because of me.

Except now . . .
I don't actually feel good.
I feel tired.
I feel sad.
I don't want to be president.
I just wanted Kate to see me.
I miss her.
Ugh.
Now I feel bad.

• •

Kate

Seriously.

All anyone can talk about
falls into two categories:

1) How cool Levi is for being the chicken head
2) How cool Tam is going to be as president

Well here's a third category for everyone:
3) Shut your stupid pie holes

Seriously.

• •

TAM

I might have hit my
high five limit
which is a thing
I did not know
I had.
But every minute
of every day
every kid
wants a smack
because of my speech
and my presidential promises
which I absolutely
cannot keep.
Ugh.

• •

Kate

If I have to hear
one
more
time
about that stupid
everyone gets a cheerleader thing
that Tam said

AS A JOKE,
I am going to catch on fire
and then possibly
explode.

• •

Kate

Can you come get me?
I text Jill.
I can't take it anymore.

What?
Skip school?
I don't think so.

is her reply,

and fine.
Fine.
So glad she's BFFs with Mom now.
So glad no one is on my side.

• •

TAM

I hate this feeling.
I hate it so much.
I only ran in the election
to get Kate's attention.
I didn't mean to screw it up.
I don't want her to lose.
I definitely don't want to win.
I'm going to take my name off the ballot.
And then
I'm going to find a rocket
and shoot myself to Mars.
I want to escape this whole mess,
get out of these halls.

• •

Alyx

Alexx

Well this is fun.

Chaos reigns.

Up is down and down is up.

Can anything else happen?

Any more wildness in store?

What will tomorrow bring?

I'm almost afraid to know.

I'm almost afraid to know.

I'm almost afraid to know.

Kate

The first one was easy
yank
rip
trash.
I never even stopped walking,
smooth,
chin high,
hiding in plain sight.

I yanked another,
I ripped another,
filled the trash in every hall.
Tam's posters crumpled,
her grins,
her blah-blah VOTE FOR MEs
shredded in the bins
looking up at me
and it was like I was watching
a brand-new Kate
take over my arms
like I couldn't believe
this girl
was doing this terrible thing
so easily
and with a smile.

I was on my way out the door
before I heard,

Douglass? What in the world?

Now I'm in the principal's office
and let's just say . . . it's not great.

• •

Kate

I don't get in trouble.
That's not a thing I do.
So watching the principal's mouth
turn into a deep, long line
while she paces back and forth
makes my brain
sting in a way
it has never stung before.

You gave such a nice speech!
This doesn't make sense!

Her hands go to her hips
as she says words like:

Irresponsible.

She says,

Really disappointing.

She says,

I thought you were
one of our leaders,

She says,

one of our best kids.

She says,

But now . . .

She says,

You're off the ballot.

She says,

That's for sure.

She says,

And you're replacing the posters.

She says,

That's also for sure.

And the words hang
in the air
thick
clinging
to my stinging brain,

Your mom is on the way,

she says,
her final words,
the worst of them all,
as I sit here
hands on my face.

• •

TAM

I should be mad.
I want to be mad
as the principal explains
Kate has been sent home.
(What!)

She will be making me
all new posters
before election day.
(What!)
And Kate
is off the ballot,
having proven
she is not a good candidate
for student council.
(What! WHAT!)
And she will have detention
for quite some time
to learn about respect
and blah blah blah.

I should be mad.
I want to be mad.
But I know I pushed her,
I know it was my fault.
I know I ruined this for her
by being a huge jerk.

I take a deep breath
and tell the principal
I don't care about the posters,
I quit the election,
whatshisname can win,
I just want all of this to be over.

• •

Kate

Mom isn't talking,
which is weird because
Mom always talks,
especially when she's mad.
But right now she's super quiet
as the car hums its way home.

It's lucky,

she says finally

the MisDirection tickets
are nonrefundable.

She looks at me.
Hard.

You're lucky
the show is tomorrow.
You're lucky
I'm too busy
to try to sell them online.

I look down at my lap.

I bought those to help you.
But no.
You don't want to be captain.
I don't know, Katherine . . .
What has gotten into you?
What is your problem?

I almost start to laugh because,
my problem?
I already TOLD HER
and she didn't LISTEN to me.

My problem is so much more
than concert tickets
I could SCREAM.

• •

TAM

Maybe I should say I'm sorry
to Kate
for the election,
for everything.

Though she was mean, too,
saying those things,
tearing up my posters.

I just . . .
if she feels as confused
as I do
then maybe we can start over.

• •

Kate

Can I come in?

Jill's at my door.
A quiet knock.

Sure.

Ready for the concert?
The big party?

I guess.

People will be getting here soon.
Might want to get dressed.

Okay.

Kate?

Yeah?

You all right?

It's my birthday.
I'm great.
I'm totally fine.

Really?

Yes!

She comes to my bed,
grabs me in a hug,
whispers,

You know I'll always love you,
no matter who *you love.*

I know,
I whisper back,
I love you, too.
And my heart caves in a little bit.
Will I ever be able to love me, too?

• •

TAM

The front door opens.

Oh.
It's you.

I don't know what to say,
I'm not even sure why I'm here
except,
You tore down all my posters.
My arms cross,
hugging my chest.

I thought you hated posters.

I roll my eyes.
Yes. You're hilarious.
Kate sighs deep
and long
like it comes from her toes.
She looks at the floor
then says,

You can't actually do
any of that,
you know.

Any of what?

The things in your speech.

I know.

Then why did you say it?
To make me look dumb?

I shrug.
I wanted to show you . . .
I don't know.

Mostly I just wanted you to
see me.

I see you every day.
Your face.
Those posters.

I laugh.
My *posters?*
You're the one who's
everywhere.

Anyway.
I'm sorry.

Why are YOU sorry?
I'm the one who threw a fit.
I acted like a baby.
I gave you the election.

I don't want the election.
I quit.

What?!
Then what DO you want?

I want . . .

There's a lot of noise,
then,
squealing,
running,
chaos
as the squad appears
behind Kate
on the stairs.

Wha—

MisDirection.
My birthday.

MDOMG, how could I forget?

She just looks at me,
her eyes red,
mouth turned down.

I don't know.
How could you?

• •

Kate

In the doorway
she looks smaller
than she ever has before.
Hunched over,
hands in her pockets,
and I'm not sure what she wants.
Except . . .
she always knows what she wants.
That's a Tam thing.
A Tam specialty.
So surely she's here for a reason,
surely she wants *something*.
She just looks at me, though,
like she's trying to remember who I am,

like she's trying to recognize my face,
like I'm a stranger
in some strange land.

• •

TAM

Why am I here again?
That's the question of the night.
How did I end up at her house
when she clearly hates me,
is clearly busy
with this birthday party
and as always
I'm extra,
in the way,
not part of the group,
ugh,
okay, Tam.
Time to go for real.
Forever.
Time to get away.

• •

TAM

The floors are finished.
I blurt,
feet frozen
for some reason,
not leaving
for some reason.

Yes.
Don't they look great?

I . . . guess?

The girls are all so loud,
shouting for Kate
to come upstairs.

I should probably . . .

Yes.
Go up there.
It's your big day.
Sorry I interrupted.

Unless . . .

Unless . . .

You probably hate me now.

Her chin sticks out,
her bottom lip
in the smallest of pouts.
Her face points to the floor,
but her eyes lift,
looking at me,

seeing me,
until my heart flips
and flops
and flips
again
and hate is not the word
I'd ever use for her.

Hate you?
Over some stupid posters?
I have a lot more reasons to hate you
than just that.

Her eyes flare wide,
her chin quivers.

Hey.
Hey.
I was just kidding.
I could never hate you, Kate.
Why would you think that?

Well,
uh,

Her eyes again.
I can't stop looking at them.
Deep, dark,
black mysteries
as she
glances behind her,
says,

Want to come in?

She's staring at the floor now,
instead of me,
her words rushed,
her cheeks pink.

Sure,
my mouth says,
before my brain can catch up.
For a minute.
But then I have to go.

Why would I say yes?
Her mom is in there.
And the whole squad.
This is a terrible idea.
But when she looks up,
her face is hopeful,
her eyes so wide,
if I said no right now,
I might actually curl up
and die.

• •

Kate

She's here,
and I have so much to say,
but the whole squad
sits in my room
chattering,

looking at Tam
out of the sides of their eyes
like
she might burst into flames
and there's just no way
to actually talk
or say anything
so I don't.

• •

TAM

The squad's MisDirection shirts,
glittering at me
make me realize immediately
this was a bad idea.

I was never meant to be here,
not for the party,
or the concert,
or even in Kate's life.

Everything about me is too different.
Too not perfect.
I will never fit
no matter how hard Kate tries.

• •

Kate

Presents!

Becca yells,
as the squad surrounds me.

The last thing I see
before the blindfold goes on
is Tam in the corner
looking completely lost.

• •

TAM

Okay.
It's time to leave.
This isn't the Kate
who was at the front door.
Her eyes fooled me
for just a minute
but now I see the truth.
The yo-yo friend is
back again
the old Kate
everyone else knows so well.

• •

Kate

Sharp light
underlines
the bottom of the blindfold
as Becca giggles
and the other girls do, too.

I yank off the blindfold
as soon as Becca yells

Okay, open!

and the first thing I see is Tam,
making her way to the door,
but she's stopped,
trapped,
by a life-size cutout of Ben,
the brooding one.

Becca squeals,
the others do, too:

We know you like the moody type!

and

You finally have a boyfriend now!

They all laugh, and
Tam starts to laugh, too,
but it's different,
harsh and loud.

She swipes at tears,
casting her glance around.
Looking at us,
at the MisDirection poster,
at giant Ben,
at me.

Her nose is running,
but she doesn't seem to care.
My Redwood,
so angry.

• •

TAM

I can't be here anymore.
I want out.
I need out.
She's clearly made her choice:
The squad.
MisDirection.
Boyfriends.
That's it.

I make it to the door, but
the cutout of Ben taunts me,
haunts me,
his pretty face
so concerned.

I flick him in the forehead,
and my mouth starts talking
before I realize it.

• •

TAM

These boys
make themselves
look
[flick]
like
[flick]
girls
[flick]
so the girls
[flick]
will
[flick]
like
them.
[flick]

Can't you see that?
Isn't that weird?

There is a dent in Ben's
perfect
forehead
now.

But if you're a girl
[flick]
who likes girls
[flick]
then the same girls
[flick]
who like boys who look like girls
[flick]
think you're *the weird one.*
[flick]

Is that what you're afraid of, Kate?
That you're the weird one, Kate?

I walk over to her.
Stand so close to her.
I can feel the bursts of her
breath
on the front of my neck,
her chin tilted up
so she can see me,
her super tall
Redwood
bearing down.

You can't be weird, Kate?
[I want to flick her forehead, but I don't.]
You can't be different at all?
[I want to flick her forehead, but I don't.]
It messes up your perfect life?
[I want to flick her forehead, but I don't.]

A stupid
horrible
embarrassing
sob
chokes out of me:

Did you ever even like me at all?

• •

Kate

The gasp is loud.
Did it come from me?
And Tam is standing
right there
practically on top of me,
breathing hard,
face streaming,
her eyebrows an angry *V*.

I don't know what to say.

Did Tam just say . . . ?
I shake my head.

My cheeks flame
as burning hot fire
climbs my whole face,

Why did you even come here today?
My voice just as fiery, just as hot.
This is a party for normal *girls, you know.*
Maybe not the best fit
for your type.

The words shoot out of my mouth,
even as my brain slows down
and I hear
what she said
over and over
again.

• •

TAM

These words shoot from her mouth
and it's like I float to the ceiling
watching her say them to me
and I wonder
wildly,
how is this even happening?

I watch from above
as tears sting my eyes
and I say as calmly as I can,

I'm sorry I'm not perfect.
But I'm glad I'm not you.

• •

Kate

What's wrong with being perfect?
I hate how my voice shrieks.

The very definition of perfection means
nothing's wrong.
And when nothing's wrong,
everyone's happy.
So why wouldn't you want that?
I hate how my tears stream.

There's nothing wrong
when everything's right,
and when everything's right
everyone is happy,
and when everyone is happy
everything is perfect.

See?

I swipe the tears off my face,
angrily.

I'm everything
everyone *in this room*
wants to be.
The perfect girl.
The perfect me.

• •

TAM

You said everyone
a hundred billion times
but you only said I *once.*
Seems to me, if you're talking about
your own happiness
you might have that
backwards.
If everyone else is happy, Ponytail,
where does that leave you?

• •

Kate

My MisDirection poster
stares at us.
Brooding Ben
stares at us.
The squad
stares at us,
and my words,
they aren't coming out right.
I can't make Tam see
that if I'm perfect
I don't have to be afraid.

I can't find the words
to tell her
the path I'm on
is perfectly straight.

I can't tell her that
if I'm the girl
she thinks I am,
I'm afraid
I'll lose everything.
And that's a lot to burn down.

• •

TAM

I can tell when you're happy
and right now, Kate, you're so sad.
But I can't tell you if you're gay, okay.
Only you can know that.

Chloe squeaks. Becca gasps.
None of the girls can stop staring.

Kate's mom has appeared,
jaw jutting out like Kate's,
hands on her hips,
but not in an adorable way.
For the first time since Kate gave it to me
I take off the bracelet,
put it in her hand.

I don't want you to be sad.
I want you to be happy, I swear.
Pretend you never met me.
Watch me disappear.

• •

Kate

I disappear, too.
Poof.
Even though the squad tries to act
like everything's normal.
But Tam is gone.
Gone-gone.
For real.
And it's like I'm not even here,
not part of the crowd,
not pulsating with the lights and sound.
It's like I'm in a bubble,
an echoing sphere
and all I hear
is Tam's voice
I can't tell you if you're gay, okay.
I can't tell you if you're gay, okay.
I can't tell you if you're gay, okay.
And all I can do is push
push
push
my way
out of the crowd

out of the light
out of the noise
into the night
where I gasp the damp air,
suck it down into my lungs
until all my guts,
all my insides
hurl onto the ground.
I cough and spit
and lose everything inside
and then I put a hand on the wall,
steady myself
and I cry and cry and cry
until finally I call Mom,
who drives straight to the show
and brings Jill, who stays with the squad
because I can't stop throwing up.

• •

Kate

On the couch at home,
bucket by my side,
I know
everyone knows
my secret now,
and it's turning me inside out.

Katherine.

Mom curls her arms around me.

Katie.
Baby.

She hasn't called me Katie
since I *was* a baby.

What did you eat?

She rocks me back and forth
and I lean into her chest.
I remember being little
with the flu
curled up on her for days,
giving her the flu, too.
And how she didn't care about the germs,
she cared only about me,
and maybe that's how it's always been,
even if she
cares in weird ways.

Mom,
I say into her chest.
(I really need her to know this.
I really need her to listen.)
It's never been seventy-five percent.
I am definitely old enough to know
I'm one hundred percent gay.

Her fingers run through my hair,
her hand cups my face.
She looks at me and says,

It's going to be okay, Katie.
You're going to be okay.

No.
I push her away
so I can look harder into her face.
What I'm trying to tell you,
what I'm trying to say is . . .

I close my eyes,
my voice shakes.

I don't want to hear it WILL be okay.
I want to hear that RIGHT NOW is okay.
Tell me this ME is okay.
Tell me I AM okay.

My liquid guts spin and churn,
cleaning out the old Kate,
and Mom kisses my head,
rubs my back,
finally says,

You know I only want the best
for you.

And I guess right now,
hearing that,
is going to have to do.

• •

TAM

I just . . .
why do I have to be ten feet tall?
why don't I fit in anywhere?
why can't I be . . . normal?
why does everything have to be so hard?

When you were born, I knew.
I knew you'd be so
wonderful, unique.
And every mom says that, sure,
but I could see it,
your light,
your energy,
burning so hot,
so bright.

No offense, Mom, but
no one else cares if I'm unique.
Unique just means strange.
Unique is not good.

I care.
Frankie cares.
Kate cares.

Well, Kate *does not care.*
She just wants to be
The Fanciest Normal.
The Normalest Normal.
And that *is a prize I'll never win*
I guess.

Oh, honey.
If you think being normal is a win,
then I have done my job wrong.

• •

Kate

Do you think you are?
Gay, I mean?
Lesbionic?

This is what Becca said to me
in my room
after the show
when she came to check on me
after Jill drove everyone home.

Lesbionic isn't a word.
I said.

I know.
But it sounds cool.
Do you . . .
do you think it sounds like . . .
you?

Yes, I guess?
Probably.
Likely.
Definitely.

My mouth was dry.
My heart beating fast.
Was she going to hate me?

Did, you, like, have a crush on me?
Is that why we were best friends,
and then not best friends anymore?

What? No!
I never had a crush on you.
Only . . .
only Tam.

She is super mad at you.

Um. Duh.

Maybe you should talk to her.

It feels too late for that.

It's only too late if you want it to be.
Buck up, buttercup.
If you like her, get her back.

Becca is gone now
and I feel really, super calm.
No more throwing up.
No more churning guts.
I can't believe I said all of that out loud.
To her.
To Mom.
And now
I can't believe neither of them
seems to hate me
at all.

• •

TAM

Since it appears I have
zero friends now,
I wander to Levi's house
to see if he hates me, too.

When the door opens,
he seems surprised,
but he invites me in,
and his brother says hi
before he disappears to his room.

Levi looks different now,
more serious than I've ever seen.
He's quieter, too.

Hey.

Hey.

There's so much to say,
and I can't speak for Kate, but . . .
That slap . . .

Knocked me back.
Dang.

He smiles, but his eyes
study the ground.

It's just . . . she works really hard,
on the mascot stuff,
on everything,

and then there you were
and it was so easy for you,
plus, I think, well,
I think she's jealous of you.

Jealous? Of me?
Why?
Because of the mascot?
Or because you were my friend
first?
I barely even see you now.
We barely even talk anymore.
It's all Kate Kate Kate Kate.
You've pretty much disappeared.

I know.
I'm sorry.
Things have been intense lately.
But you're still my shortstack, right?
My man about town?

I want to be.
You're still my nerd, right?
My giant goofball?

He throws a video game
controller at me,
and we sit on the couch and play.
No more words,
only arm punches and laughs,
just like the old days.

• •

Alex	Alyx	Alexx
What do we have here?		
	Something interesting?	
		A breakthrough?
Watch closely.		
	Our Ponytail.	
		Eyes open.
She finally sees.		
	Her eyes are wide.	
		Her heart grows.
What will she do now?		
	She can fix it.	
		Where's her Redwood?

Kate

I admit
I didn't want to come to school
today
or ever
again.
Not after MDOMG
took OMG
to an
entirely
new
level.

But here I am.
In the hall.
Waiting for . . .
what?
Lightning
to strike me down?
The squad
to revolt?
The whole school
to laugh at me
for not being like everyone else?

Those are definitely most of the things
I'm standing here waiting for,
but something else I know
is that my chest is tight,

my breath is caught,
and my heart is pounding
at the thought
that Tam is here somewhere
and she hates my guts right now.
She has no idea that
since the last time we talked
I've turned
inside out.

• •

TAM

I want to see her.
I don't want to see her.
I want to talk to her.
I don't want to talk to her.
I feel itchy and terrible
knowing she must hate me now.
I feel exhausted and sad
that I said those things
in front of her whole squad.
But I also feel like
she forgets I'm a real person
with real feelings
and not just some girl
she can be friends with
when it fits into her schedule.
I want to see her.

I don’t want to see her.
I want to talk to her.
I don’t want to talk to her.
I’m twisted in knots.
I hate it so much.

• •

Kate

Lunch.
Now what?
Sit with the squad?
Sit all alone?
What does the real Kate want?

The real Kate wants to go home.

• •

TAM

Lunch.
Now what?
Levi’s with me.
Kate’s with her squad.
Business as usual.
Except . . . no, it’s not.

• •

Kate

The squad talks about the show,
tells me how sad they are
I missed most of it.
They don't say anything about
the rest of the night,
the birthday to remember.

I try to listen.
I try not to look over
at Tam and Levi's table.
I try not to wonder what
would happen
if I walked over.

I try to distract myself.
Here, let me see that.
I set down my sandwich,
wiggle my fingers.
Becca protests, but I wiggle
harder.
Come on. I won't hurt it.
You never get to be in any pictures.
Sit down.
I'll get you with the group.

She sighs and sits by my lunch bag
and I take three steps back,
hold the camera up,
yell,

Yearbook!

snap snap snap
and when I push the arrow button
to make sure the pictures aren't blurry
I scroll back
and see a bunch of older pictures.
Kids in the halls,
Kids on the bus,
Kids at a play.
Me and Tam at lunch.

I stop.

The picture is from a distance,
my head is tilted to the side,
my eyes
on Tam
as she laughs,
her face so open,
so bright
and right now I forget where I am.
The world drops away.

My breath catches,
my tummy twists,
this
picture:
Tam, so full of light.
Tam, reflected in my own eyes.
Redwood and Ponytail
quiet
in the wild.

And suddenly I get it.
I really do:
why you might want to
make a picture bigger,
make it poster-size,
hang it on your wall,
stare at it every day,
maybe slide your hand
across its surface,
try to absorb it into your skin.

Like a kick to the stomach,
I feel Tam's pain,
I get it now,
I understand
why my giggling
at the MisDirection poster
made her so mad.

It wasn't that she was angry
about a stupid band,
it's that her feelings were hurt.
She wanted me to act that way
not because of them,
but because of her.

I swallow hard.
I walk out into the hall,
my pounding heart
out of control.

Kate!
Where are you going?
Kate!
I need that camera back!
Kate!

NOW

Kate

There's an explosion of white foam,
loud whooshing
shooting
from the canister in Mom's hands.

Just like that,
the fire is out.

What on earth . . . ?!
Katherine . . . ?!

Foam drips from the wall,
big splats
onto the floor,
the oak
that gets more say in this house
than I do.

I need to see Tam,
my voice is strong
familiar
coming from deep within,
I'll be right back.

Oh, no, ma'am.
You are not leaving this . . .
Katherine!
Get back here!

• •

TAM

Kate

What do you want?

To see you.
To talk to you.

What if I don't want to?

Please.

What if I'm done?
With games.
With everything.
With you.

Tam.
Please.

• •

Kate

TAM

I'm estimating
one hundred and fifty percent.

One hundred and fifty percent?

Gay.
I thought you'd like to know.

• •

TAM

Very interesting.

• •

Kate

That's all you have to say?

• •

TAM

[shrug]
[fighting off a tiny smile]

• •

Kate

Also.
I made two things for you,
since it appears
you lost your bracelet.
Ahem.
First . . .

TAM

You made me a phone?

A video, silly.
Don't look at me like that.
Just watch it.
Please.
It's breaking news.

And she watches it.
And her face
goes slack,
her mouth hangs open,
making me laugh.

You burned *the MisDirection*
poster?

You told me it was okay
if I burned it all down.

I didn't mean it that way!
MDOMG!
Kate!

But also, I did this.

I hand her a long tube.
She crinkles her brow
as she reaches in,
pulls out a new poster.

I made two.

She looks at the poster
then looks at me
then looks at the poster again
then her smile is huge.

When was this taken?

I don't know.
Early in the school year, I guess.

Look at you.

Look at you.

Look at us.

Look at us.

Come on.
I have the perfect place for it.

• •

Kate

She tacks the poster of us
right there on her bedroom wall
and I talk
and talk
and talk some more.

I had a plan,
you know?
A list
with little boxes
to
check
check
check.

But the little boxes danced around
and I couldn't catch them with my pen.
My check marks flailed,
turning into birds
with lopsided wings
disappearing
leaving me with no plan
no list
no boxes
no check marks
no plan
did I mention no plan?
No plan.
I have no plan,
Tam.
I have no plan.
Not anymore.

• •

Kate

We walk back to my house,
pinkies swinging,
and I don't care if Mom sees
or what she thinks.

Tam's Muppet voice says,

I've missed you,
little pinkie.

My Muppet voice says,
I've missed you, too.

Mom seems frozen in the kitchen,
all fancy and brand-new
as Tam and I go upstairs
to my still-smoking room.

Oh, man,

Tam says,
seeing the black spot on the wall.

Look what you did.
Yikes!
And . . .
Wow.

But wait.
There's more.
Check this out . . .
I laugh as I yank an old drawing
right off the wall.

I take the drawing
out of its frame,
grab some push pins,
Tam laughs,

No way!

I hang the frame
around the scorch on the wall.
Looks like I felt my feelings,
thanks to you
and Levi
and the squad
and Mom.

• •

TAM

Hours go by.
We talk
about moms
and Jill
and Levi.
About plans
and lack thereof
and impulse control.

We talk about holding hands
and what that means
and maybe it means nothing
or maybe it means
everything.

We talk about that forbidden word
the tiny word
that fills both our heads
and how we'll figure out
our words
one day
all on our own.

We need our own word,
you know?
A phrase
just for us.
Because you're not my best friend
or my best girl
or my girlfriend
or my whole world
you're something even bigger, Kate.
Bigger than just one word.

• •

TAM | **Kate**

She's my winning point.
She's my summer day.
She's my sneaky wink.

She's my cheering crowd.
She's my laugh out loud.
She's my secret smile.

She's my light.
She's my heart.

She's my Kate.
I'm her Tam.

She's my Tam.
I'm her Kate.

Together
we're everything.

• •

Maybe we should meet again.
Start over, brand new.
Redwood and her Ponytail,
a second first day
at school.

TOMORROW

TAM

Over there,
she thinks I don't see
but I do,
I do,
that little cheerleader
looking at me.
The red bow in her hair
snapped military tight
right?
Like she must've used a ruler
and glue
and maybe an iron, too
to get that perfect
swoop
on top of a perfect
swinging
ponytail
like I've never seen
swish swish
catching the light
blinding my eyes
that snappy red bow
those bright highlights
like
what
excuse me

are you on purpose
bringing every dream of mine
to life?

• •

Kate

This girl today,
looking at me.
Tall as a palm tree,
shaped like one, too.
Big hair on top,
giraffe neck,
legs like a stick figure
stretching right off the page,
her skin shimmering
her head tossed back
a loud laugh flying from her mouth
while she looks over at me
winks
and I feel like
a final piece
in a puzzle
just fell into place
making sense
of it all.

• •

TAM

Kate

The little cheerleader
from earlier
saunters up,
eyes twinkling bright.
What's your name, Ponytail?

My name is Kate.
What's yours?
Redwood?

Cause I'm so tall?
Hilarious.
My name is Tam.
Short for Tamara.
But I have to put you through that basket—
I point to the court—
if you ever call me Tamara.

Nice to meet you, Tam.

Nice to meet you, Kate.

I wink

She winks!

and I offer my hand.

I take her hand.
Hold it tight.

And right now,
in this moment

And right now,
in this moment

I feel like I've known her
my whole life.

• •